Ghost Stories

Ghost Stories

by Jack Ross

99% Press,
an imprint of Lasavia Publishing Ltd.
Auckland, New Zealand

Sources & Acknowledgments:

Cover image - Graham Fletcher:
Detail from 'Untitled (Red, Yellow and Blue)' (2018), by courtesy of the artist.

Several of the pieces included here have been previously published, sometimes in revised or truncated form. A complete list has been provided at the back of the book. Thanks are due to the editors and publishers of those anthologies, websites and journals for permission to reproduce them here.

ISBN: 978-0-9951165-5-9

**when a house is haunted
it's one's own ghost that
invites the others in**

Cao Xueqin,
The Red Chamber Dream

Table of Contents

Introduction

The Classic New Zealand Ghost Story

I recently read a book called *Hauntings and Apparitions: An Investigation of the Evidence*, by New Zealand-born writer Andrew Mackenzie. It's a kind of compendium-cum-analysis of a number of cases collected over time by the British Society for Psychical Research, from a series edited by Brian Inglis, one of the true heavyweights in the paranormal field.

It's certainly a substantial and scholarly book, but perhaps the most important thing in it comes near the end, where Mackenzie reports a conversation he once had with Rosalind Heywood:

> When I first started writing about apparitions I made the mistake of studying them in isolation, rather than as part of the structure of psychical research as a whole. ... talking over the subject with Rosalind Heywood, particularly during the last year of her life, my outlook gradually changed. I eventually realised that instead of asking, 'What is an apparition?' I should be asking, 'What is man?' It was as if we were discussing the nature of shadows instead of the nature of who or what casts the shadows. When I put this conclusion to Mrs Heywood her reply was 'But of course'.

In other words, the most important thing about any haunting, or supernatural experience generally, is *who* it happens to. It's rather like dream interpretation: there's no way of decoding dream symbols until you find out what they mean to the person who's had the dream. And if they won't tell you, there are still a few ways of finding out.

Taking a couple of basic Freudian rules-of-thumb as our guiding points, then:

We assert most vociferously that which we're least certain of.

The claim: 'I'm a brilliant teacher,' for instance, can be translated more accurately as: 'I secretly suspect I'm a terrible teacher.'

We're most haunted by that which we've worked hardest to deny and eradicate from our lives.

Rabid homophobia, for instance, is generally understood to mask strong homoerotic tendencies (as in the movie *American Beauty*).

This central principle of the *return of the repressed* may help to explain the preponderance of native agency in the ghost stories recorded in post-colonial countries.

On the one hand, for the coloniser, the intense guilt of having dispossessed someone of all control and ownership of their lives tends to make you portray them as full of sinister purpose and secret knowledge.

On the other hand, for the colonised, there's a certain advantage to playing up to this scenario. When you lack power in one world, you're forced to assert it in the other. Hence the large numbers of tohungas, obeah men, voodoo priests, and even – going back a bit – druids who allegedly channel access to the other side (not that there may not be substance to their claims).

Anyway, reading Mackenzie's book got me to thinking a bit more about the local product. Here are a few samples I myself have collected:

1970	Robyn Jenkin. *New Zealand Mysteries*. 2nd ed. Fontana Silver Fern. Auckland & London: Collins, 1976.
1978	Robyn Jenkin. *The New Zealand Ghost Book*. Wellington: A. H. & A. W. Reed.
1998	Grant Shanks & Tahu Potiki, eds. *Where No Birds Sing: Tales of the Supernatural in Aotearoa*. Christchurch: Shoal Bay Press.
1999	Grant Shanks & Tahu Potiki, eds. *When the Wind Calls Your Name: Tales of the Supernatural in Aotearoa*. Christchurch: Shoal Bay Press.
2005	Julie Miller & Grant Osborn. *Ghost Hunt: True New Zealand Ghost Stories*. Auckland: TVNZ / Reed.
2007	Julie Miller & Grant Osborn. *Unexplained New Zealand:*

      Ghosts, UFOs & Mysterious Creatures. Auckland: Reed Publishing (NZ) Ltd.

2015   Mark Wallbank. *Voices in the Walls – Living the paranormal in New Zealand*. Auckland: Haunted Auckland.

2016   Mark Wallbank. *Talking to Shadows – A New Zealand paranormal research team's search for answers*. Auckland: Haunted Auckland.

I guess one's first observation might be that such books seem to come in pairs, perhaps because they generally elicit such an unexpectedly enthusiastic response as to spawn a sequel, but then the essentially sterile and repetitive nature of such narratives becomes apparent, and the impulse dies.

The second point might be that each compilation reflects the prevailing view of ghosts, and – more importantly – how to conduct psychic investigations, prevalent at the time.

Robyn Jenkins' two books are standard pieces of journalism, collecting well-known, though undoubtedly intriguing, feature stories about the Tamil Bell, the Spanish helmet and other old chestnuts. They are clearly meant as contributions to an essentially regional, folkloristic view of the paranormal as a source of local identity.

The two books by Julie Miller and Grant Osborn are dominated by the format of the very entertaining, though not particularly convincing, TV series that gave rise to them. Once again, the model here is successful overseas reality shows such as Yvette Fielding and Karl Beattie's *Most Haunted* (2002 to present) in the UK, and Jason Hawes and Grant Wilson's *Ghost Hunters* (2004-2016) in the USA.

The two recent books by Mark Wallbank and his team from the *Haunted Auckland* website come from a more internet-dominated, less edited or structured approach. The emphasis here is on recording every detail, however trivial, in the possibly vain hope that it will eventually amount to something.

By far the most interesting among this set of books are, to me at any rate, the pair edited by Grant Shanks and Tahu Potiki. They seem to take the most original and homegrown view of the subject. Perhaps because they have set out simply to collect a series of allegedly true experiences contributed by many different people, with minimal editorial intervention, it is really only in these two books that one begins to get a glimpse of what might be called the classic New

Zealand ghost story.

The story runs essentially as follows (no one story in either book has all of these features, but very few are without one or two of them):

> A young family, a farmer, or a long-lost relative of some old family moves into a new house / farm / estate. They promptly start to make changes or improvements, ignoring all warnings from neighbours / locals.
>
> Manifestations start to appear. These can take the form of a string of bad luck, shadowy presences in the house, or just a general feeling of depression and doom.
>
> Things start to get so bad that they are forced to ask for help. Someone from the district offers to have a word to the 'old people' at the marae.
>
> A group of elders duly appear, walk the land, recite a few words, and the trouble recedes. This may be accompanied by the restoration of a bone, a grave or an artefact which has been tampered with somehow.
>
> Thereafter, everything runs more smoothly, in an atmosphere of mutual respect.
>
> Alternatively, the farmer, or *pater familias*, refuses all help, and is either forced to move away or dies in mysterious circumstances (an upturned tractor, perhaps – or a septic wound).

First of all, one should note the strong focus on haunted *spaces*, rather than haunted *people*. These spaces can include houses, and farms, but also patches of bush (as in the title story of Shanks and Potiki's first book, 'Where No Birds Sing'), river valleys, and mountain passes: wild, deserted areas, essentially.

The problems generally start due to some breach of tapu, deliberate or accidental. Entering a forbidden area or, particularly, removing a bone or a piece of carving from its seemingly accidental location in a sand-dune or old tree-trunk leads to dire consequences.

In almost all cases the people in trouble have to talk to someone *local*, who brings in some elders from a nearby marae or, occasionally, further afield. They walk through the space and speak karakia, and everything settles down.

The alternative to this is death in suspicious circumstances for the unrepentant farmer who's ploughed up a tapu area, or city-slicker who won't, or can't, return a valuable artefact.

The phenomena mentioned in these stories include giant eels and dogs as well as haunted patches of bush, mysterious fires, and time-slips. *All* are seen to relate to Māori folklore, in one way or another.

A colleague told us recently about a walk he took with his girlfriend. They started off quite late in the day, and couldn't reach the hut they were planning to stay in. Instead, they pitched their tent in an inviting piece of bush. The place made them feel so uncomfortable, though, that they just couldn't stay there. So they packed up the tent and walked on until they reached the hut. Later, discussing their experience with another tramper, they were told that the place they'd stopped in was tapu. His girlfriend in particular was quite shaken by it. He said that there was no possibility of remaining: the imperative to leave was just too strong.

Some friends of my parents once told us of an experience they had while boating on Lake Taupo, when they discovered some old cliff-paintings and artefacts. The day immediately clouded over and the waves got so high that they had to wait for some time for them to subside before they were able to get home. Everything had been sunny and bright until that precise moment.

What is one to say to such 'authentic' experiences? Perhaps just that we more recent immigrants to New Zealand can never be quite unconscious of what Sam Neill, in his classic documentary *Cinema of Unease*, refers to as 'the dark, threatening land.' Or perhaps Allen Curnow said it even better in 'House and Land' (1941), referring to the 'great gloom' that:

> Stands in a land of settlers
> With never a soul at home.

Stories

My mind on other things, I said that **The Red Badge of Courage** *was 'a great ghost story in which the ghost never appears'.*

Peter Straub, Ghost Story

Eketahuna

I had to drive from Wellington to Auckland.

I'd left it till pretty late in the day to start, for various reasons: a meeting that didn't come off − quite a frustrating set of encounters, actually.

Anyway, the net result was that I was pleased to be back on the road, but wanted something more interesting than just the usual grind up the Kapiti coast, then across the volcanic plateau to Taupo.

Instead, I thought I'd drive through the Hutt valley, over the Rimutaka ranges to that line of small towns on the other side, and up the east side of the island. I'd never gone that way before, and it looked quite attractive on the map.

I knew that there was no way I'd be getting home that day. I know people talk about pulling all-nighters and driving up from Wellington in one go, but I know myself that I simply lose concentration after a few hours behind the wheel, and no amount of ten minute breaks or quick cups of coffee will revive me enough to keep on going after that.

Once or twice I've actually nodded off behind the wheel, but that's another story − the fact that I'm telling you this one shows that I survived it. Just barely, though.

So there I was, driving along that road north of the Rimutakas, as the sky gradually began to go dark, starting to think about where I might find to stay for the night.

On previous drives I'd once or twice set up my tent in a rest area. There was a bit too much noise and hooning around for me to get much sleep, though. Nobody actually broke into the tent, but next morning I found the side-mirror missing from my car. I suspect I must have had quite a narrow escape. So it was a motel or a campground I was looking for, or perhaps a B & B.

After a while the signs started to say 'Eketahuna,' and I got to thinking about that name. I remembered that years ago some would-be humorous columnist had started a campaign to deny the existence of Eketahuna, and even claimed that he'd travelled to where it was marked on the map and found nothing whatsoever there.

It was a laborious jest, and nobody really fell for it, but I do recall a number of indignant Ekethunans writing in to assert the objective existence of their hamlet, and denounce snooty Aucklanders who dared to poke fun at solid heartland citizens.

Anyway, part of my cult of never planning things in advance – a reaction to my childhood, when every trip and expedition was plotted and prepared for to the nth degree months before it happened? – was being at the mercy of just such passing whims.

Why not stop in Eketahuna? I thought. It would have a certain cachet to sleep in a bona-fide ghost town, one whose very being had been called into question. It seemed like a funny idea, and I could already hear myself telling the story at dinner-parties in the future. Even if the place was completely boring, that too could form part of the joke.

So on I drove, closer and closer to that elusive Eketahuna.

I must have reached there around six or six thirty p.m. It was late in the year, and the lights were already on up and down the main street. It was not yet completely dark, but certainly shading off into night.

There was no-one there. I know that sounds odd. I've already mentioned the lights being on. Those things were there, yes: shops, petrol stations, lamp-posts. All the trappings of yet another 'blink and you've missed it', 'road-goes-through-to-somewhere-else' transit towns. Just no people. Anywhere.

I drove down the main street fairly slowly, looking around. Not a soul in sight. I guess they must all have been inside, watching the 6 o'clock news. Or worshipping the great god Dagon, for all I know. In any case, the lights were all on but no-one was home. It was a kind of Mary Celeste town, spooky and atmospheric, yes, but a little disconcerting to someone hoping to find shelter for the night.

But there it was! A sign. A sign that said 'motorcamp,' pointing off down a sidestreet. Just what the doctor ordered, I thought. I'll go down and find the motorcamp, and see if they've got any cabins to rent. Somehow the idea of pitching a tent in the darkness that was coming on so rapidly just didn't appeal.

After a couple of hundred yards, the sealed road turned into a gravel one. A couple of hundred yards more, and it became a dirt road. Literally. There was a little cardboard sign pointing through a fence into a field, saying something like 'Murchison's campground.'

There didn't seem much alternative, so I started bumping the car through the potholes and hummocks of an old farmtrack.

I was just about to give up, and write the whole thing off as a will o' the wisp, when the car came up over the brow of a hill and I saw, down a steep slope, the Eketahuna campground.

There was an old concrete utility shed in the middle of a muddy field. The ground was strewn with pineneedles and pinecones, as there were trees scattered through it. There was not a soul there (unsurprisingly), but I could see that, in season, a hardy wilderness camper could probably pitch a pup-tent somewhere down there. As long as they had a four-wheel drive to get down the slope and were reasonably confident about being able to drive up it again.

Turning my car around was no easy task. Finally I had to back up to about halfway through the field and then reverse very gingerly onto some tussock in order to get back onto the track. That field was muddy, I can tell you, and my confidence in finding a friendly farmer to tow out my car had sunk to an all-time low.

Now, why on earth would you leave up a sign saying 'campground' on the main street of your town, when all that sign led to was a muddy field in a pine forest, with, admittedly, a toilet block sitting there proud and tall for all to see?

And even if that was a mere oversight, why would you open the gate to the field, and leave up the tattered sign which constituted the next turn in the maze? I have no answer to these questions. I didn't feel disposed to ask any locals just at that moment – full dark had declared itself by now – though it still intrigues me to this day.

The most urgent priority at that moment seemed to be shaking the dust of Eketahuna off my feet. So that's what I did. I drove back into town, took a sharp left, and hooned off out of there, being careful to observe the exact speed-limit, mind you, I've seen too many road-movies with scenes of unspeakable things being inflicted on passing motorists by bored highway patrolmen.

I felt no desire to encounter any of their Eketahunan kinsmen. For all I knew they might eat human flesh. Certainly the evidence of the motorcamp sign showed that they had a lively sense of humour, and possibly a bit of a grudge against city slickers to work off.

So there I was, back in my car, zooming along the highway, full headlights on, wondering where the hell I was going to stay for the night. Somewhere a long way from Eketahuna seemed the best bet.

I even toyed with the idea of keeping on until I got back to Auckland. It was only a few hundred miles, after all. I knew, though, that I simply wouldn't be up to it. Sooner or later I'd end up drifting off the road, either deliberately or involuntarily, and I really didn't fancy another night stretched out across the back seat in some out-of-the-way rest area.

It still wasn't all that late, though; and by now I'd put a good few miles between me and the shadow over Eketahuna, so when I saw that lit-up 'motel' sign I thought that all my Christmases had come at once.

It was in the middle of the most blah, nothing place you can imagine. A road, a flat horizon, not that I could see very much of it in the dark – no other buildings or signs of a town anywhere around.

But the sign did say 'motel,' and there weren't any other offers on the table, so I turned into the parking-lot and parked outside the office. The lights were all on outside, lighting up the raw anonymous brick of the empty courtyard, but I couldn't see any signs of life within.

I rang on the doorbell. No answer.

I rang again. A vague creaking sound came from inside. Then nothing.

Again. This time I could hear definite stirrings and signs of movement.

Usually you get a blast of whatever's playing on TV when the proprietor comes out into the office to book you in for the night, but there was none of that this time. Nor was there anything particularly picturesque about the guy who opened the door to me.

He looked as flat as the bricks of his house, a kind of man-composite, neither large nor small, old nor young, fat nor skinny.

'Could I have a room for the night?'

No answer.

'You've got your "vacancy" sign lit up.' *Kind of appropriate, really*, I might have added, as he chewed over the import of this complex set of sentences.

'Out the back,' he said, finally.

I was going to say 'grunted,' but he didn't really sound them that hard. It was more like the words had no savour in his mouth – as if he was simply reading them off a card, or reciting them from some distant memory.

'My car? You mean, park it out the back?'

He nodded. 'Come back for the key.'

It's not like any of this is unusual. We all know the drill about stopping at these highway motels and motorcamps. The manager generally has something else going on in the house that they're anxious to get back to – dinner, or a video, or their favourite programme, and it's actually kind of a relief that they're seldom anxious to shoot the breeze with you. This guy did seem a bit over-laconic, though, like he was in danger of losing sight of the basic need to make a living renting units if he took it much further.

Anyway, be that as it may, I got back into the car, drove it round behind the house, then returned to find a key lying on the mat outside the door. He hadn't even charged me, let alone told me where my room was, but the number was written on the key and I guessed he must be a trusting soul. Either that, or just too bored with the whole business to care whether I went zooming off in the morning, having stripped the place bare.

I don't recall what number room it was. It's tempting to call it '13' and make the whole thing sound spookier than it was. There weren't many rooms there, though, just a single line of them on the far side of the courtyard, so I guess it was probably something like three or four. Maybe even number one. Who knows?

It wasn't too hard to locate it, unlock the door, check out the generic furnishings and pretty much collapse into bed. I didn't have the energy even to make myself a cup of tea, let alone go foraging for anything to eat. I promised myself a slap-up breakfast at the first town I came to in the morning, but I just couldn't face another conversation with mister faceless in the main office.

The sign on the door had said something about milk in the morning, so I hoped I might be able to make myself some instant coffee then, at least. Enough to get me back on the road, anyway.

It's funny how hard it can be to get to sleep when everything around you is dead quiet. It's just not an experience one encounters in the city. There's always some light, some noise coming from somewhere. You learn to filter it out, to fall asleep anyway, but then, when it isn't there, somehow you miss it.

That's what happened to me, despite being so dog-tired to start with. The blackness outside was as thick as velvet, the silence almost palpable. After a while I realised that I needed something to react against, so I tried putting in earplugs so at least I'd have the slight tinnitus they bring on in your inner ear.

That worked better, much better. But it also means that I'm still not sure if I was fully asleep or just dozing fitfully when it happened.

Someone was shaking me. I had a vague memory of having heard some voices, even of a kind of dark figure looming over the bed, but this was unequivocal. I was being shaken awake.

'Wake up! Wake up!'

A voice was shouting at me, but it came through muffled, only half-audible. The earplugs! That was why. I tried to sit up, to swim up into full consciousness.

There was a woman standing beside my bed. She wasn't shaking me anymore, but I had to presume that she was the one who'd been ordering me to wake up.

'Wha ... What's going on?'

I'm seldom at my best when woken in the middle of the night. Maybe some people spring up out of bed fully conscious, ready to face any peril, but I'm not one of them.

'What are you doing here?' she asked me.

By now I'd taken out the earplugs, so I could hear pretty well. Luckily I hadn't stripped down completely before going to bed, but I was still conscious of being only half-dressed, in t-shirt and underpants.

'This is my room. I rented it for the night.'

'You rented a room,' she repeated. 'But how did you get in here? Did you just break in?'

'No, of course not,' I replied. By now I was starting to feel a bit angry. What the hell was this strange woman doing, in my bedroom at night, asking me all these stupid questions? 'I got a key from the guy in the house. He told me to park around the back, and then to come back and collect it.'

'He – told – you – to – park – around – the – back,' she repeated.

'Yes, that's right,' I said. 'Why? What's the problem? Was he not supposed to? Are you not taking guests at the moment?'

The whole thing was sounding stranger by the moment. Who was this woman? His wife? His daughter? Was she mad, or touched somehow? Or was it the old guy himself who was a couple of sandwiches short of a picnic?

It was a bit hard to see why she looked so surprised by it all, though. It was a motel, after all. How anomalous could it be to find a guest sleeping in one of the rooms?

'What did he look like, this "man" you're talking about?'

'Look, I don't have the faintest idea what's going on here, but I just drove in to rent a room for the night. I didn't break in, and I picked up the key from the old man in the most normal way possible. If there's a problem with me staying here, then I'm happy to drive on instead, but you can hardly expect me to pay for the night if you won't let me sleep here. He acted like he had every right to rent me a room, and there's just no way I could have known if he was supposed to be letting me in.'

I subsided, slowly, as I saw that she wasn't really listening. The expression on her face, which I'd interpreted before as rage or indignation, I now saw to be an extreme tension bordering on fear. She was looking around the room as if she couldn't quite believe what she saw here, couldn't compute what was going on.

'Who the hell is he? Who are you, for that matter?'

'I'm his daughter,' she replied, in a rather milder tone than she'd used up till then.

'So you didn't know he was renting out rooms behind your back? I take it this is your place, not his?'

'No,' she said, softly. 'You see, he's been gone for two years.'

'Gone?' I said. 'You mean, shot through, disappeared?'

'I mean gone. Dead. He's been dead for two years now.'

'That's impossible ... An old man, kind of stringy looking? Sandy hair?'

'Yes.'

'Well, it must have been somebody else, then. Someone else who was in the house, and who gave me a key to this room.'

'Who?' she said.

'How could I know that? A neighbour, a friend, someone with a sick sense of humour.'

'It was him,' she said simply. 'What did he actually say to you, do you remember?'

'He said "round the back" – and he kind of nodded at the car. That was it, basically.'

'It was him. I know it. I've never seen him myself, but some other people have. At first I thought they were just having me on, but I guess I can't really keep that one up any more.'

'You're the one who's having me on,' I said. 'This is just some trick you play on the tourists. I suppose you've got a video camera playing behind the mirror, or something like that.'

'No,' she said simply. She must have been in her mid-thirties, I suppose, kind of heavyset but not unattractive. She didn't look the type to sustain such an elaborate practical joke, if you know what I mean. And yet.

'I don't believe in ghosts', I said, somewhat futilely, under the circumstances.

'Neither do I,' she replied, 'but who else could it have been? Nobody lives around here but us ... But me', she corrected herself. That little correction rang true, to me. She was quite used to living there in the house, with her Dad. The idea that he was still ushering in random motorists to stay in their units was definitely shocking to her, but not, somehow, entirely beyond belief.

'I'll leave you to sleep, then,' she continued.

'You'll leave me to sleep! How the hell do you think I'm going to get to sleep after what you've just told me? With either your Dad's ghost or some psychotic neighbour wandering around?'

'I'll leave you to sleep.'

She was receding now, into the darkness of the room.

It struck me, then, that she'd never turned on a light at any point during the conversation. The lock clicked as she went out, clattering slightly as she pulled out her pass-key from the other side of the door.

The whole thing seemed stranger and stranger, the more I thought about it, and there wasn't much else to do, alone in that strange little brick-tile motel room. It just didn't add up, somehow. Why had she come in to accost me like that? I might have been dangerous, after all, especially if I had broken into the unit.

How could she have missed my car, parked safely, I hoped, behind the main building? Why hadn't she woken me up by turning on the main light in the room? The simplest explanation: that she was a little bit crazy, seemed by far the most logical one as I thought through what she'd told me.

The ghostly motel-owner had looked just rather spooky. I remembered again just how curiously flat he'd seemed. But a loony daughter flitting from room to room in the dark made a lot more sense.

You wouldn't believe that I got any sleep after that, but I did. For all I know the whole thing was a dream, though it didn't seem like one – far too solid and circumstantial.

I woke up with a start to the sound of birds outside the window. Only then did it strike me that she could have crept back into the unit and cut my throat in my sleep. She did have the run of the whole place, after all. She'd seemed a gentle soul, mind you – not the homicidal maniac type – but then for all I know that could be one of the distinguishing characteristics of psycho killers.

I sure as hell wasn't going to wait around for any early morning milk deliveries. I'd unpacked very little the night before, so I was back in my clothes and out the door a couple of minutes later. The sun was up, and for the first time I could really see just how flat and boring and lonely a spot this was.

There was no answer at the door when I knocked on it. I did feel tempted just to jump in the car and hoof it out of there, but some kind of strange residue of childhood conscience constrained me. There wasn't anything as useful as a scale of charges up on the door, so I compromised, finally – after knocking and shouting a few more times – by leaving forty bucks under a stone by the doormat.

Maybe I short-changed them, maybe not. It wasn't much of a night's sleep, that's for sure, but I have to say that I'm very glad I paid for it, all things considered.

There was a rural café a wee way down the road, and luckily it was already open for business: early risers in the country, I guess. The proprietor seemed a chatty sort, and as I was ordering my coffee and eggs, he asked me where I'd been staying.

'Oh, a motel a couple of miles back down the road. Brick place, with a couple of units out the back.'

He looked at me a little strangely, and said 'Where did you say? You mean, back in the town, thirty, forty miles back?'

'No, no,' I continued, half-disposed to give him the whole yarn. 'I guess it must have been some kind of farm: a house and a couple of units beside the courtyard.'

'On the main road? This road out here?'

'Yes.'

'There's no motels round here. Not fitting that description, anyway. You're sure it wasn't a B & B? Roses round the door, old couple?'

'No, no, nothing like that – there was a big 'motel' sign out the front. It had a big lighted up VACANCY on it. It was kind of a strange place, though.'

'Strange how?' he asked.

'Well, it was an old guy who let me in, but then I met his daughter later, and she seemed to think that there was something funny about that. I couldn't quite work out why.'

I found myself consciously shaping and abridging the story as I told it. I didn't want to blurt out any of the ghost story she'd told me, but nor did I want to close him off from confirming it if there was something in it – some kind of local legend.

'Mister, I don't know where you think you've been staying, but it can't have been in the place you're talking about.'

'You do know it, then?'

'Of course I know it. That old farm, house, units. It's been up for sale for more than six months now. It must have been the big FOR SALE notice you saw.'

'But who's living there?'

'Nobody's living there.'

'Well, maybe one of the neighbours has been renting out rooms in there on the sly.'

'I doubt it. Not after what happened.'

'What did happen?'

'After the fire, I mean.'

I suppose that's where I'd leave it if this was just a piece of fiction. But since it isn't, it doesn't end so neatly.

I tried to question the guy further, but he seemed to have lost his appetite for conversation by then. I gathered that there'd been a fire on the farm a couple of years before and that most of the buildings had been gutted.

'Except the units?' I asked hopefully. He wouldn't confirm or deny that one – just glared at me sideways.

'An old man and his daughter?' I asked again. He nodded, glumly. 'And where are they now?' I asked.

'Both dead,' he replied.

And that was that. I could have driven back up the road to take another look at the motel, I suppose, but it was going to be a long day's drive in any case, and I somehow didn't really want to see the picture he was painting for me.

I still don't have the faintest idea what happened to me that night – a dream I suppose, or some very inventive gossip from the town wag in the café, but I did learn one thing: don't scoff at what you don't understand.

And remember that you never quite know who you're talking to, especially in an old house on a dark night somewhere near the exact dead centre of nowhere.

The Scam

I'd sat down to rest for a moment, when I discovered I was being addressed. A pleasant-looking, not-too-old not-too-young woman had asked me where I was from.

'New Zealand,' I replied.

'Oh, I thought America.'

This led to more desultory conversation. She was from Manila, staying with cousins, as her brother worked here in Hong Kong (more of *him* later). In fact, he, the brother, was planning a trip to New Zealand, so could I perhaps oblige with some details of where to go, what to see, etc.?

I did so, to the best of my ability, though she scarcely seemed to be paying attention. I asked her to recommend a good cheap place to eat. She obliged, then asked if I would be averse to meeting her brother later, after lunch, to tell him some more about New Zealand and Australia, having previously ascertained that I had no particular plans for the afternoon.

'Why not?' said I, my suspicions aroused. What if this were a scheme for drawing me into some back alley, compromising, or coshing, me, then running off with my hard-earned traveller's cheques?

Nevertheless, when one o'clock came round, I was in the appointed place. Why not, after all? 'Open to experience' – Kendrick Smithyman's mantra. It might be interesting, at least.

My acquaintance Gaby arrived a moment later, and led me off the main drag, down many smaller streets, to see her brother. He lived in a tiny room off an apartment filled with Filipino maids.

'They are here for a Christmas party. Their one day off. Domestic servants,' she said.

From the moment we entered the room her brother Joe took charge. He sat me down and, with a combination of judicious questions and fluent chatter, segued into a most interesting subject: his aunt, who was suffering from leukaemia, and the money required to keep her in a nearby hospital. All the time he was chain-smoking little, pencil-like cheroots – the room was full of overflowing ashtrays.

To look after his 'patient,' as he called her, he was forced to promote card-games even on his rare days off. Last night they'd been playing Mah-jongg till four in the morning, and that morning he'd taken $US 2,000 to the hospital. His *real* job, however, was as a dealer in a casino, where with his 'special skills' he protected the house's interests. Enforcer? I asked myself. He didn't look strong enough. The pay was good, but he needed more, and for this had taken on a partner, a black man, to whom he gave thirty percent. The partner was now growing greedy, though – wanting fifty percent. Soon it might rise to seventy percent.

And how did their particular scam work? Why, just out of interest, just to show me, you understand, he would illustrate. A table was quickly set up: cards, mah-jongg counters, and the lesson began. How do you win at poker-blackjack? Why, the dealer shows you the next card as he shuffles them. The chances of this escaping the camera monitors seemed slim, but that was the reason for the thirty percent which went to his superior, he explained. This is not enough, though. You must also know what is in the banker's own hand – in the hidden card-bunker.

closed fist = 10
thmb and forefinger = 6
ring and little finger closed = 5

We practised. I made mistakes. He corrected them. All was going swimmingly.

At this point another person appeared, a rather portly, cheerful Thai businessman. The Mah-jongg game was due to start at four p.m., and the guests to arrive from three thirty onwards. *This* guy had turned up at two twenty, elated by having won so much, 16,000 US dollars, he boasted, in the previous night's game.

Joe immediately started a spiel about how much I'd lost to him that morning, in order to promote a game of poker. Was this the real scam? With mounting terror, I saw the cards being set up, money produced, the possibility of big losses from my non-existent investment.

'My sister can play – you watch,' he said to me, having drawn me aside to discuss the new deal in the walk-in shower. However, when he required my signature on a statement of the stakes, I decided it was time to decamp.

Gaby showed me the way out, and we parted with a few general and insincere words of farewell. I might have won thousands of dollars if I'd persevered with his tuition. I'd have lost far more in sheer anxiety, though.

※

What a classic mark I must look! Travelling alone, bumbag and tourist appurtenances, dopey expression. On the way back to the hotel I was accosted by a bearded Indian who told my fortune with much circumstantial mumbo-jumbo: 'One who is close to you is very false, sweet to your face, not in the heart. You very good man, think too much, do very practical work, very hard.'

I left him to it when the subject turned to money. Enough is really enough.

Featherston

'It's just a little thing called – the Constitution!
Just a little thing a lot of people died for.'

Mr Smith Goes to Washington is – or, rather, used to be – one of my favourite films. So it came as a bit of a surprise to me the other day, when, watching it again for the umpteenth time, I found the quote above, intoned by Jimmy Stewart in the middle of his filibustering attempt to stop the passage of a fellow-senator's crooked land-appropriation bill, had *entirely disappeared*.

There's a lot of talk about lost causes, 'the only kind worth fighting for,' as Jefferson Smith murmurs before lapsing into unconsciousness; there's even a section where Smith picks up a copy of the United States Constitution and starts to read it aloud – but no line resembling, 'it's just a little thing called the Constitution,' can be heard from beginning to end of the movie.

And yet I *remember* it. I can even hear Stewart saying it, in his inimitable bumbling drawl. Where did it go? Are there two versions of the film? Did it disappear on the cutting-room floor, or during the transition from one medium, film, to another, DVD? I have no explanation to offer. I've had to stop quoting the lines to people as they appear to have no external reference point beyond my own mind.

✳

A couple of years ago my then wife and I went for a drive north of Wellington, over the Rimutaka ranges and through the small towns beyond. Greytown, Carterton, Masterton, between them they contain a lot of antique and second-hand shops. We looked in what seemed like all of them. On the way back, in the late afternoon, we stopped briefly in Featherston.

I knew little of Featherston except the name. Afterwards I realised that it was the site of *Shuriken*, Vincent O'Sullivan's 1985 play about the infamous Japanese 1943 prison camp massacre, but that didn't even occur to me at the time.

There was a little bookshop on one side of the square, with a sign on the front mentioning opening times, but the door was locked. Peering in through the dusty window, we could dimly make out a huge stack of books on top of a table in the centre of the room. Everything else was bare and deserted. The shop looked not only shut, but as if it had been flooded out, or stripped in preparation for the movers. The sign continued to maintain blithely that it was open for business, though.

Moving on further around the square, we found a combination second-hand / junk shop. There was a light on inside, and the door opened when we pushed on it, but there were no other signs of occupation. Certainly there was no-one at the glass counter in the middle of the room.

Perhaps 'warehouse' might be a better description than 'shop'. The place was vast! It included racks of books, videos, fabrics, plates, furniture – you name it, it was there. We started to wander around and look at things in a desultory manner. It all looked very old and dusty and untouched.

It took some time for us to realise that there was something wrong with it, or at any rate something very odd. It started for me when I glanced at the rack of videotapes. None of them looked particularly pristine, but the point is that all of the titles were *entirely unfamiliar* to me. Not the genres, mind you: there were plenty of screwball comedies, kung fu movies, self-help tapes. Just not the same ones I'd seen before. Nor did any of the actor's names ring a bell.

Can this really be? I wondered. How could there not be a single familiar film among so *many* tapes and titles? My curiosity aroused, I began to rummage through the cheap paperbacks and romances. Same thing. They looked familiar enough superficially: slim candy-coloured spines like Mills & Boons, great fat bodice-rippers like Angelique or Wilbur Smith, but *not* any of those authors or series – just the same sorts of books.

Most disturbing of all were the records, though. I don't usually make a habit of leafing through boxes of LPs – who has a record player nowadays? – but these record sleeves were *weird*. There were old New Zealand bands from the 70s sitting on logs around campfires, with titles like 'Banjo got my Soul' or 'Ti-tree Anthems'. I don't know much about pop music, but I felt that I might have noticed some of these shaggy characters if they'd ever been on television back in the day. Not a one of them was familiar to me *at all*.

It was as if the shop had come out of a completely different space-time continuum – one very close to our own, close enough for the same kinds of drivel to be peddled in bookshops and record shops, but just different enough for there to be a *complete discontinuity* in specifics. Similar in genus, completely different in type.

At this point I realised we were being watched. There was a man standing behind the glass case of the counter. Where he'd come from is unclear to me to this day. Could he *really* have walked out from the back, through all those ranks of shelves and aisles, completely unobserved by either of us? I guess he must have, since the only other alternative was that he had simply materialised there. Unless there was a hidden staircase down there behind the shelves of dusty glassware.

He was the *stillest* man I think I've ever encountered. He hardly seemed to breathe, and I'm not sure that I saw his eyes blink even once during our brief conversation.

'Can I help you?' he said.

'Oh, no, just browsing,' I replied. Cassie just stood there, as if transfixed with terror. She told me afterwards that all the cloth samples she'd bought in the shop were ruined somehow when she got them home. They'd looked all right *in situ*, but when you unrolled or unpicked them, stained or creased beyond the point of repair.

'You're not wanting to close, are you?' I continued.

He didn't move. Or answer. So we kept on poking around. Not for long, though. The creepy vibe of the place had begun to get to both of us. We had visions of being ushered out the back and getting one sight of Bluebeard's bloody chamber before the axes started to descend. Worse, of a stainless steel umbilicus leading up to a waiting spaceship.

Nothing happened, though. Cassie bought her few rolls of fabric: rather more pricey than one might have expected for so sorry a specimen of the genus 'Op Shop', but still costing only a few dollars in all. I was tempted to buy a few books or records, but something in me seemed to say no. *This* was their rightful place, and they should not be taken from it.

We went out into the street, leaving the lighted windows of the shop the sole illumination over Featherston's whole town centre. Nothing had *happened*, exactly, but it felt as if we'd had a narrow escape.

To this day I've never been back there. I doubt I could retrace my steps even if I wanted to. I seriously question if the shop we entered that day was of this world.

There are universes all around us, say the Physicists: dark matter and superstrings and instantaneously disappearing-and-materialising quanta. What wonder, then, if from time to time we take a wrong turning in the midst of our seemingly stable world?

Leaves from a Diary of the
End of the World

The world was so recent that many things lacked names, and in order to indicate them it was necessary to point.

Gabriel García Márquez,
One Hundred Years of Solitude

Tuesday, 21 February, 2012

Today I found an old book in the library, in the de-accessioned pile. It cost me two dollars to buy it (**Hardback Non-fiction** – if it had been **Fiction**, it would only have been a dollar). The title was *Breaking the Maya Code*, by Michael Coe.

But why on earth were they throwing it out?

It's true that this was a copy of the *first*, 1992, edition, and since then – I checked – Coe has gone on to publish a number of revisions of his book, just as he did with his 1966 text *The Maya*, now in its eighth edition. So perhaps they thought it was too out of date to be useful.

What *I* suspect, though, is that they read those words 'the Maya Code' as something analogous to *the Da Vinci Code*, as a reference to the, alleged, Mayan Prediction of the end of days in December 2012.

If so, they were sorely mistaken. Far from an Occultist text full of babble about the Apocalypse, Coe's is a profoundly scholarly work, which tells the tale of one of the great decipherments in history.

The name of Yuri Valentinovich Knorosov, the Russian genius whose phonological and comparative methodology finally led to success in this two-hundred-year-old quest, should undoubtedly go down in history along with Jean-François Champollion, Michael Ventris, and other heroes of the intellect.

The fact that we can now actually read these texts from a far-off civilisation, mute for centuries, thanks solely to such feats of ingenuity is one of the few proofs I know that the cosmos is not entirely arbitrary.

Just as the patterns of Nature become clear over time when examined by the dispassionate intellect, so advances *can* be made in our knowledge, the stones *can* be made to speak.

Funnily enough, when I tried to find the book again to verify these references, it had disappeared into the jungle of my too well-stocked shelves. Perhaps because its work was done; perhaps because paying too much attention to the glyphs themselves might become, in its turn, a distraction from the main event: the culmination of this present cycle of ours.

⚶

Monday, 8 October, 2012

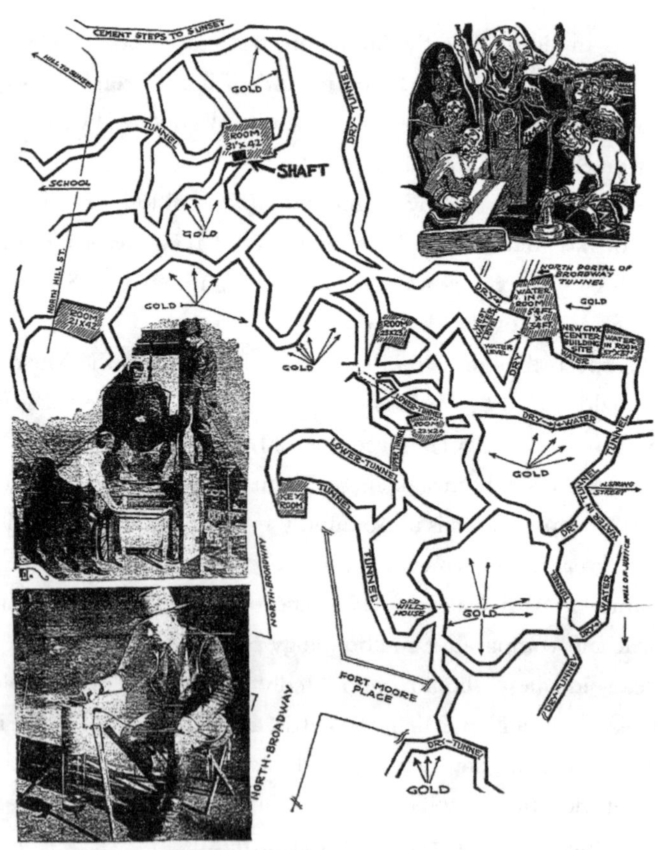

This is a map of the tunnels of the Lizard People under Los Angeles.

That may sound a bit unlikely. I'm sure you've all heard about the tunnels under North Head, full of old wartime ammunition dumps, as well as the two first Boeings ever built, but the idea of 'lizard people' probably strikes you as coming straight out of Science Fiction.

There really *was* a cover story about them in the *Los Angeles Times* for January 29, 1934, though. A mining engineer claimed to have discovered traces of them with a 'radio X-ray' device he'd built to detect 'minerals and tunnels below the surface of the ground.'

Further details came from a Hopi Indian chief in Arizona, who told him that the tunnels were the remains of one of three lost cities built after 'the 'great catastrophe' which occurred about 5000 years ago':

> This legendary catastrophe was in the form of a huge tongue
> of fire, which 'came out of the Southwest, destroying all in it's
> [*sic.*] path ... the path being several hundred miles wide.' The
> city underground was dug as a means of escaping future fires.

Interestingly, the engineer, G. Warren Shufelt, disappeared shortly after this article appeared, and has never been heard from since.

1934 AD [the year the article appeared] – **'5000 years'** [the approximate time elapsed since the fiery 'catastrophe'] **= 3066 BC**

It seems a bit more than a coincidence that this date is within *less than fifty years* (forty eight to be precise) of 3114 BC, the, alleged, date of commencement of the fourth creation in the Mayan count.

If we measure back from 2012, we can see just exactly how far Shufelt's discovery was ahead of its time: seventy-eight years, to be precise. Perhaps that's why he had to disappear: if people had known that another catastrophe was coming, they might have panicked and run amuck, as they did a few years later, after Orson Welles' infamous radio adaptation of H. G. Wells' *War of the Worlds* in 1938, on the brink of the Second World War.

⚑

Wednesday, 23 December, 2012

Michael Coe ends *Breaking the Maya Code* as follows:

> The Maya wise men all across Yucatán predict that the world will end in the year 2000 *y pico* – 'and a little.' How many years will that 'a little' be? The Great Cycle of the Maya calendar which began in darkness on 13 August 3114 BC will come to an end after almost five millennia on 23 December AD 2012, when many of you who read this will still be alive. … And what is to happen? A Katun prophecy in the Book of Chilam Balam of Tizimín reads:

Ca hualahom caan	Then the sky is divided
Can nocpahi peten	Then the land is raised
Ca ix hopp i	And then there begins
U hum ox lahun ti ku	The Book of the 13 Gods.
Ca uch i	Then occurs
No hai cabil	The great flooding of the Earth
Ca lik i	Then arises
Noh Itzam Cab Ain	The great Itzam Cab Ain.
Tz'ocebal u than	The ending of the word,
U uutz' katun	The fold of the Katun:
Lai hun yecül	That is a flood
Bin tz'oce(ce)bal	Which will be the ending
u than katun	of the word of the Katun

It's pretty clear from this that the catastrophe will take the form of a *flood*.

And so it has.

Is it any accident that even the most conservative predictions have the sea-levels rising between fifty-six and two hundred centimeters (22 or 79 inches) during the 21st century? Whereas the melting of the Greenland and Antarctic ice sheets, could contribute four to six meters (13 to 20 feet) *or more* to present levels.

Try to imagine what that means the next time you go to the beach. First add seven feet, the height of the tallest man, to the high tide levels you see marked on the sand. What would be left of the coastal community behind you? Then expand it to twenty feet. What would remain of the surrounding towns and suburbs?

The end is near, make no mistake about it. As with the lost land bridges between the straits of Gibraltar, the Bosphorus, the waters will flow in gradually, but the result will be a new sea: a new Mediterranean, a new Black Sea. We may not see it yet but it *is* coming. Our futile attempts to hold it off were always that: futile.

Better, instead, to beat the bounds of the new dispensation: learn to read the signs of the coming age in a hundred everyday things.

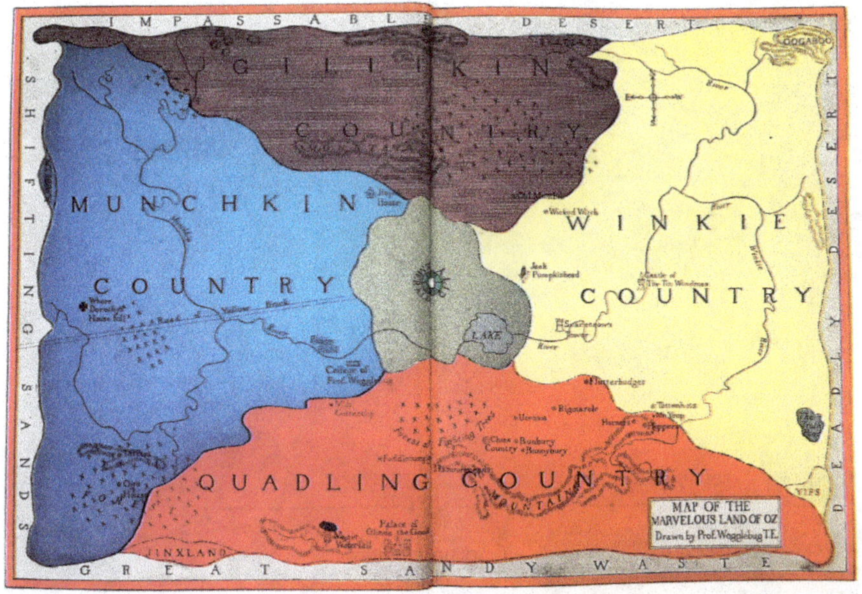

✸

Sunday, 6 January, 2013

I was struck today, while reading L. Frank Baum's *The Marvelous Land of Oz*, by the following passage. Tip, the young boy who will be transformed into a girl, 'Ozma', at the end of the story, explains how you can always know exactly where you are in Oz:

> ... in the Emerald City everything is green that is purple here. And in the Country of the Munchkins, over at the East, everything is blue; and in the South country of the Quadlings everything is red; and in the West country of the Winkies, where the Tin Woodman rules, everything is yellow.

There's even a map included in the endpapers to illustrate the idea.

The Maya, too, saw each of the four directions as governed by a particular colour. Admittedly they were slightly different from L. Frank Baum's, but the basic concept was the same:

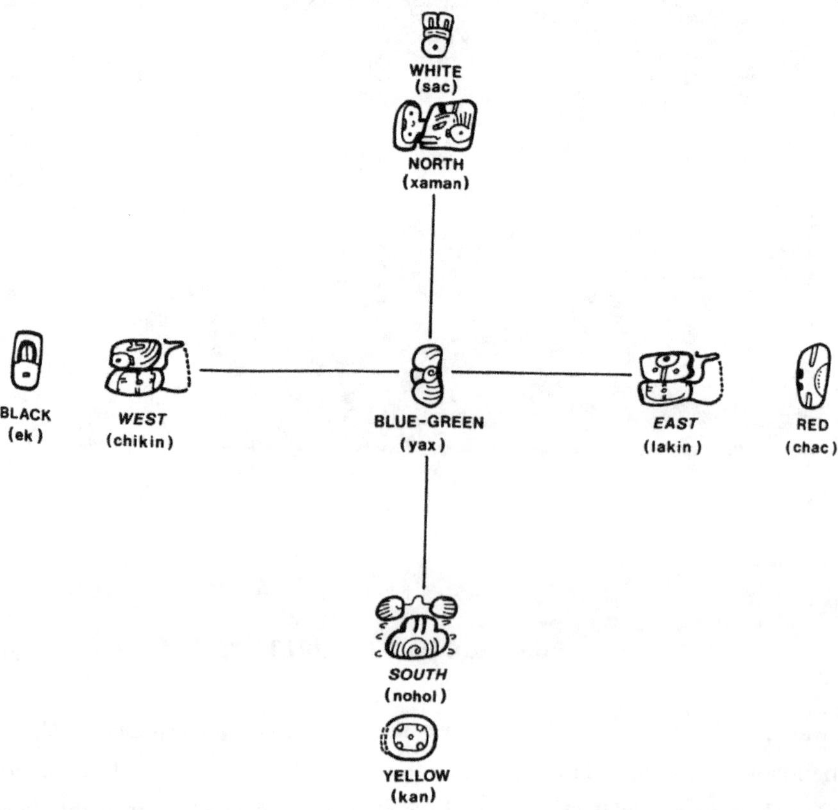

White for the *North* – of ice and snow; **Red** for the *East* – where the sun comes up; **Black** for the wild oceans to the *West*; **Yellow** for the deserts of the *South*, with **Bluegreen** at the *Centre* – for the lands of men.

Michael Coe's book *The Maya*, which I took this picture from, goes on to explain some of the principles behind their multiplicity of gods:

> Exceedingly little is known about the Maya pantheon. That their Olympus was peopled with a bewildering number of gods can be seen in the eighteenth-century manuscript, 'Ritual of the Bakabs,' in which 166 deities are mentioned by name, or in the pre-Conquest codices where more than thirty can be distinguished. … *First*, in the case of certain gods, each was not only one but four individuals, separately assigned to the color-directions. *Secondly*, a number seem to have had a counterpart of the opposite sex as consort, a reflection of the Mesoamerican principle of dualism, the unity of opposite principles. *Thirdly*, some seem to have had young and old aspects, or (especially in Classic times) fleshed and fleshless guises. *Fourthly*, there was no clear dividing line between humans and animals, or even between species of animals, so that many supernaturals combine these elements in fantastic ways. And *lastly*, every astronomical god has an Underworld avatar, as he died and passed beneath the earth to reappear once more in the eastern sky. [*my emphases*]

Young and old, male and female, fleshed and fleshless – it's like that thought experiment of placing grains of wheat on a chessboard. One grain goes on the first square, two on the second, four on the third. Before you reach the sixty-fourth square, the grains of wheat you need will outnumber all the atoms in the universe.

Or all the words, the names, in every human language?

For Tip to become Ozma, the sexes, like the sky, must reverse. Are there other lessons concealed in Baum's books, frivolous though they appear on the surface?

Is there something encoded there about *self-sacrifice*, like the 'spotless virgin' in the **Mayan** hunting song?

✹

Wednesday, 6 February, 2013

I've had this little paperback for years: *La literatura de los Mayas*: Mayan Literature. There's a companion volume of Aztec Literature. They're both in Spanish, published in the 1960s.

I was looking through it the other day when I came across this poem. It was collected from among the Lacandon Maya tribesmen by a couple called Phillip and Mary Baer, and published by them in the Academic Journal *Tlalocan* in 1948:

Lacandon-Maya Poem

Every time I lift my foot
every time I lift my hand
     I shift my tail

I hear your voice from far away

I'm searching for a fallen tree
    tired now
I'll fall asleep on the fallen tree

My skin
     My ears
          my hands
            my feet
are scratched

– Demetrio Sodi M.. *La literatura de los Mayas*. 1964. El Legado de la América Indígena (México: Editorial Joaquín Mortiz, S. A., 1974): 81.

Lad Satig
Sünt

Le Viz
Mosters

Finnegan
whats
Flowing of Men
Denis Breedler
A Sad Med
Zup

Be Bold with Bananas
Gravity's Rainbow

Bat candelabra

Mosto a Marselle
The Cosmic
Script

Book pyramid

I was walking along Jervois Road, away from Ponsonby – Pon-*snobby*, they call it – when I happened to glance in the window of an art gallery.

There were five pink shelves there, each with ceramic books, pyramids, and candlesticks balanced on top of it. The artist seemed to have taken all the things she'd read and turned them into pottery statues of themselves: there were titles like 'Monster und Menschen in der Maya Kunst' and 'Lord Smoking Squirrel's Cacao Cup.'

I've made a little sketch-plan of the layout.

• One of the candlesticks had Adam and Eve reaching up into a tree for the forbidden fruit, with the serpent hovering above them.
• Another one had a lot of leaves attached to its branches, each one with the word 'leaf' written upon it.
• There were a couple of strange melty-looking books with candle sticks growing out of them.
•Most striking of all, there were stacks of clay books in the form of Mayan pyramids.

I wanted to go inside and ask the artist about her work, but there were a lot of guests milling around with drinks in their hands, together with the other two artists in the show, and I could see that some of them were already looking at me as if I shouldn't be there, even though I was just standing outside in the street looking in.

I could hear some of what they were talking about, though:

It's a terrible film [*someone was saying*].

Terrible? What do you mean? It's fantastic! Priestesses in flowing white robes, Sean Connery in leather, Civilisation vs. Barbarism, and then there's that bit where he's in the library, looking at the books, and the penny finally drops: ZARDOZ, their god, is really the **WIZARD** of **OZ**, so then he goes mad and starts tearing the whole place up.

But it's so *cheesey*.

'I've seen it myself!' I wanted to shout at that point. On late night television, years ago. Every time there was an ad break you'd see that motif of the great floating face turning to show the priestesses inside. But I didn't dare. They all looked too cool.

I could see that *she* knew, though. I guess that must have been the artist herself. *She* knew about Oz, about the Mayans, the whole kit and caboodle. *She* wasn't putting down the movie *Zardoz*, or laughing in other people's faces. I wish I could have talked to her about it, but I wasn't ready. Not just then, anyway.

And I would have especially liked to take some pictures of her beautiful works on my phone, but I know that gallery people don't let you do that, I've been told off for that before.

What I *felt*, though, looking in on her show, was a fierce pleasure in finding this proof that I wasn't the only one who knew that others were already at work, outlining the new order, laying out a new heaven and a new earth where male can be female, up can be down, the serpent a hero and the pyramid a book.

Thursday, 14 February, 2013

Tzotzil-Maya Prayer

Green fire
aërial fog
    be epilepsy
yellow fire
    be epilepsy
north wind
    be epilepsy
    narcolepsy
white mist
    be epilepsy

I repel it
    repel it nine times
I expel it
    expel it nine times
pacify it
    pacify it nine times
Lord

in an hour
half an hour
fly away
into the fog
fly away
as a butterfly

Slow your big pulse
slow your small pulse
both of them
within the hour
half an hour
So be it
Lord
send it away
over thirteen mountains
over thirteen hills
stop at thirteen rows of rocks
stop at thirteen rows of trees

– Demetrio Sodi M.. *La literatura de los Mayas*. 1964. El Legado de la América Indígena (México: Editorial Joaquín Mortiz, S. A., 1974): 89.

Tuesday, 12 March, 2013

There's an ad today on the University of Auckland website:

**Oxlajuj B'aqtun:
not the end but a new beginning for Maya,
Indigenous Peoples and the Earth**

On 21 December, 2012, Maya communities across the Americas
celebrated the end of the Fourth Era and welcomed the Oxlajuj

B'aqtun, the Fifth Mayan Era. The Maya Calendar is the oldest extant calendar on the planet, with a 5,200 year cycle of remarkable accuracy and complexity. However, across the planet, from the US to Russia, citizens panicked at the idea that the world would end 'as predicted by Maya astronomers'. This was a Western invention; this change does not predict the end of time but promotes continuity at a time of crisis. In his talk, Professor Arias will explain the workings of the Maya Calendar, the celebrations last December, and the way indigenous peoples throughout the Americas understand this momentous event as a starting point to reconfigure an ethical beginning for their own people, to promote an indigenous worldview on Earth, to advance decolonial processes, strengthen indigenous cultures, and protect Mother Nature in significant ways.

Could that actually be true? *Did* the world come to an end on 21ˢᵗ December 2012, the end of the thirteenth b'ak'tun in the Mayan Long Count. Professor Arias claims that 'this change does not predict the end of time but promotes continuity at a time of crisis.' But what does that mean?

People still seem to be walking around, conducting their business – loving, dying, praying, giving birth – just as they have been since August 11, 3114 BC, when the present era began.

A few points to remember:

All this has happened before: three times, in fact. However, according to the *Popol Vuh*, the Holy Book of the Quiché Maya, ours, the fourth creation, is the first wherein the gods have succeeded in keeping humans and animals alive for any length of time.

Secondly, note the close coincidence of that date with Sunday, October 23, 4004 BC, Bishop Ussher's 17ᵗʰ century calculation for the exact Date of Creation, still to be found in many old Bibles – admittedly there's a difference of 890 years, but that's surely a permissible deviation, given the tentative nature of the evidence.

After all, John Lightfoot, Ussher's predecessor, calculated the beginning of things at 3929 BC; the Talmudic scholar Yose ben Halafta at 3761 BC; the

Venerable Bede at 3952 BC; the French scholar Joseph Scaliger at 3949 BC; the Cosmologist Johannes Kepler at 3992 BC; and Sir Isaac Newton at c. 4000 BC. All within cooee of the Mayan figure.

It reminds me a bit of Gabriel García Márquez's Macondo, in *One Hundred Years of Solitude*, after the epidemic of insomnia that afflicted the early settlers:

> At the beginning of the road into the swamp they put up a sign that said MACONDO and another larger one on the main street that said GOD EXISTS. In all the houses keys to memorizing objects and feelings had been written. But the system demanded so much vigilance and moral strength that many succumbed to the spell of an imaginary reality, one invented by themselves, which was less practical for them but more comforting.

'Thus they went on living in a reality that was slipping away, momentarily captured by words, but which would escape irremediably when they forgot the values of the written letters.'

🐾

Tuesday, 19 March, 2013

'You can see that paint is going to peel off in a couple of years. I know they used to market that stuff as permanent-coat, one size fits all, but that's not really practical in a climate like this.'

'We *did* tell her at the time. She wouldn't listen, though.'

'So she was a bit of a gardener, was she?'

'Back in the day, yes. Not after the cataracts got really bad. And she found that walking down to the shops was getting harder and harder.'

'A bit like my Dad.'

He pauses, groping instinctively for a rollie from his front pocket, then remembers he'd agreed to give up a couple of years ago now. The reflex still won't quite quit.

'I ran into my brother in town one day. I mentioned that I'd been summoned upcountry for yet another deathbed scene. "So the old man's still dying," he said. And that was right. It must have been a good fifteen years of phone-calls to come up and see him for the last time. And then one day it actually happened.'

'Not my Gran. She was pretty cogent right up to the end. She checked herself into a rest-home, got rid of all her stuff, piece by piece. I've still got a few of her books lying round.'

The two men look down at the inlet below, framed by dark-green trees.

'I guess she knew all along what 'permanent' means …'

Saturday, 23 March, 2013

Yucatán-Maya Hunting Song

Hunter from the mountains
hunt
    at the edge of the grove
once
    twice
        dance
three times

Lift your face
look carefully
    make no mistake
about your prize

Have you sharpened your arrows?
Have you strung your bow?
Have you stroked your shaft
    with catzim resin?
Have you greased your arms
        your feet your knees
        your calves your ribs

                    your waist your chest
          with buck-deer fat?

Lap three times
the coloured stone
where the spotless virgin
          youth
is tied

First   run
          second
take your bow
nock your arrow
against his chest

shoot him
– not so hard as that! –
          let him suffer
as God wills

Lap again
the blue-green stone
shoot him again
but don't stop dancing
that's how we measure
          warriors
men pleasing
in the eyes of God

The sun breaks through
the eastern trees
the archer starts to sing
          his song

learning to be

a warrior

learning to run and dance

and kill

– Demetrio Sodi M.. *La literatura de los Mayas*. 1964. El Legado de la América Indígena (México: Editorial Joaquín Mortiz, S. A., 1974): 34-35.

🐾

Sunday, 14 April, 2013

'Dear me!' said Jack. 'I'm getting confused with all this history. Who is the Scarecrow*?'*

L. Frank Baum, *The Marvelous Land of Oz* (1904)

'Citizens of the sweet hereafter.'

That's what the girl says at the end of one of my favourite films, *The Sweet Hereafter*, made in Canada in 1997.

She's sitting by a ferris wheel, I think, or some kind of fairground ride.

The film is about a small town where a school bus goes off the road and gets trapped under the ice of a frozen lake, so most of the children in the community are drowned. For the rest of them, the survivors, it's as if time has stopped. All they can think about is what they've lost.

In another way, though, nothing can touch them now: the worst has already happened, and anything they can think of doing seems futile in advance.

The girl, played by Sarah Polley, has been disabled by the crash, and has to get around in a wheelchair. It's as if she's re-enacting the fate of that one child left behind by the Pied Piper in Robert Browning's poem.

She's a singer, too, at one point she sings a song with the repeated refrain, 'Courage!'

She needs quite a lot of courage herself, because, on top of everything else, she's being sexually abused by her father.

It's hard to explain why that film had such a strong effect on me when I first saw it. I know it sounds pretty dark.

Now, though, when I think of *us*, picking ourselves up and dusting ourselves off after the End of Days, I think of that girl, that town of people caught in the sweet hereafter, where all bets are off, all the rules have changed, and – new Adams, new Eves – we have to find the courage somehow to start naming the strange new things we see.

Is it Infrareal or is it Memorex?

Roberto Bolaño's *Savage Detectives*

and the Eternal Avant-garde

Mexico City, July 1982

Someone had to call Ulises's mother, I mean it was the least we could do, but Jacinto didn't have the heart to tell her that her son had disappeared in Nicaragua … just like Ambrose Bierce … and Pushkin, except that in Pushkin's case his wife … was Reality, the Frenchman who killed Pushkin was the Contras, the snows of St. Petersburg were the empty spaces Ulises Lima left in his wake, his lethargy, I mean, and his laziness and lack of common sense, and the seconds in the duel were Mexican Poetry or Latin American Poetry, which … were silent witness to the death of one of the best poets of our day.

– Roberto Bolaño, The Savage Detectives

Auckland, April 2006

Dear Leicester,

Not that I suppose you've been missing it exactly, but I thought you might like to hear some old-fashioned, Auckland-style literary goss about a few of your old friends.

So there we all were in the little Art Gallery in Northcote: comfy sofas, cushions, tables of wine and cheese. The plan was that we should each read for five minutes, then have an interval with music, then read again for another five minutes, then there would be an open mike, necessary to get funding for the gig, apparently.

In shambles Donald, just before the readings begin. He looks a bit pasty to me, and has obviously had quite a bit to drink. He asks if I can give his magazine *Bread* a bit of a puff. I say of course, but suggest that he read something himself later on in the open mike. I'm quite keen on some of the poems he's been writing recently. He likes the idea, and goes off to get some copies of the mag from Craig's car, which is parked nearby.

Meanwhile the reading begins: read read read, yawn yawn yawn. Then the interval. I talk to Craig, who says he hasn't seen Donald for quite some time, since he went off to look in the car, in fact, and is a little worried about him. 'He was popping anti-depressants in the car, and he's been drinking all day, and he was in hospital this morning with some cuts he'd made on himself.' Ah.

✳

Mexico City, May 1977

Our visceral realist activities after Ulises Lima and Arturo Belano left: automatic writing, exquisite corpses, … masturbatory writing (we wrote with the right hand and masturbated with the left, or vice versa if we were left-handed), madrigals, poem-novels, sonnets always ending with the same word, three-word messages written on walls ('This is it,' 'Laura, my love,' etc.), outrageous diaries, mail-poetry, projective verse, conversational poetry, antipoetry, … poems in hard-boiled prose … parables, fables, theatre of the absurd, pop art, haikus, … Bloody poetry (three deaths at least), pornographic poetry (heterosexual, homosexual, or bisexual, with no relation to the poet's personal preference) … We even put out a magazine … We kept moving … We kept moving … We did what we could … But nothing turned out right.

– Roberto Bolaño, *The Savage Detectives*

The reading recommences. The first two do their sets, the third begins … I'm standing to one side when in comes Donald. He *does* have copies of the latest *Bread*, but seems very unsteady on his feet. He comes up to me and asks if he can read. I suggest that I'd better do it for him, as he doesn't look like he's in very good shape. We're just discussing the matter when he starts to fall over, unfortunately on the bare feet of the wife of one of the more senior poets present, who is sitting right next to me.

'You just stood on my feet! I have a bad toe!'

'Sorry,' mutters Donald, 'Bad knee.'

At this point he starts to go over again, and I grab him to try and steady him.

Suddenly the senior poet is on the scene. 'You just stood on my wife's foot! You should get out of here!'

Donald protests, organisers start to cluster round.

'This is a paid event … You have to leave.'

'I've paid already,' says Donald, 'I don't see why I should leave.'

The senior poet seizes him and starts to thrust him towards the door. Donald resists. Others start to join in. 'What's going on?' says Hilda, as her interminably dull reading about an alcoholic failing to resist the booze meanders on.

Mexico City, November 1975

The night before … Ernesto San Epifanio had said that all literature could be classified as heterosexual, homosexual, or bisexual. Novels, in general, were heterosexual, whereas poetry was completely homosexual; I guess short stories were bisexual, although he didn't say so.

Within the vast ocean of poetry he identified various currents: faggots, queers, sissies, freaks, butches, fairies, nymphs, and philenes. But the two major currents were faggots and queers. Walt Whitman, for example, was a faggot poet, Pablo Neruda, a queer. William Blake was definitely a faggot. Octavio Paz was a queer, Borges was philene, or in other words he might be a faggot one minute and simply asexual the next. Ruben Dario was a freak, in fact the queen freak, the prototypical freak.

In *our* language, of course, he clarified. 'In the wider world the reigning freak is still Verlaine the Generous.'

– Roberto Bolaño, The Savage Detectives

🐾

The senior poet, to do him justice, is clearly experienced in such matters and by now has Donald all the way to the door. Jack stands there like a stuffed dummy thinking how unnecessary this all is and wishing they'd stop fighting with one another. Craig and the friend he came with are trying to drag Donald away. Various impotent attempts at a fist-fight between Donald and the senior poet. Shouts, curses, suddenly a wine glass comes flying through the door (presumably thrown by Donald) and detonates in the middle of the floor, luckily touching no-one.

'Shut the doors!' shouts my colleague Myra. 'That way they can't get back in.'

By now the Mayor of Northcote, who used to be a cop, has got involved. The organisers are ringing the police. The senior poet and various other bystanders come back in. Calm settles in again, as Hilda's dreary reading continues. She's started again at the beginning, lest we should have missed any of her words of wisdom.

🐾

Mexico City, November 1975

At Don Crispin's request, I talked to him about visceral realism. After he'd made a few observations like 'realism is never visceral,' 'the visceral belongs to the oneiric world,' ... which I found rather disconcerting, he theorized that we underprivileged youth were

left with no alternative but the literary avant-garde. I asked him
what exactly he meant by underprivileged ... But then I thought
about the tenement room Rosario was sharing with me and I
wasn't so sure he was wrong. The problem with literature, like
life, said Don Crispin, is that in the end people always turn into
bastards.

– Roberto Bolaño, *The Savage Detectives*

龘

The senior poet's as happy as a dog with two tails. 'Didn't think I still had it in
me. He was soft ... took mercy on him, but I could have dropped him easily with
a single punch ...' etc. etc. to anyone who'll listen.

Hoping that Donald & Craig & co. have pissed off and driven away, I do
my bit of the reading, though the audience has thinned considerably, and
understandably, by this time. The broken glass is mopped up, (relative) peace is
restored.

And now the cops come driving up. 'Why have they brought them back
here?' asks Myra. Waves of rumour come and go among those of us who are still
hanging around. It seems that the mayor pursued the malefactors in his car with
a cellphone, directing the cops where to intercept them, an event which finally
took place in the park at Stokes Point.

Craig, as he tells me later, elected to take the heat while Donald and an even
drunker member of the group took off to hide under the piles of the Harbour
Bridge.

龘

The review ... tried to sum up the [writer]'s personality in a few
words:

Intelligence: average.
Character: epileptic.

Scholarship: sloppy.

Storytelling ability: chaotic.

Prosody: chaotic.

– Roberto Bolaño, 2666

⁂

By now the organisers appear to have worked out that it's *my* friends who've been causing all the ruckus, so I think it best to leave before the cops can start questioning me and demanding addresses. On the way out, though, I encounter Craig. The cops simply let him go, as he hadn't really done anything wrong. They seem pretty bored with the whole business, in fact. The irony is that nothing would have happened if the Mayor hadn't happened to be there, and hadn't happened to be an ex-cop.

But now comes the clincher. I write to the organisers next day apologising for the disruption of their event in such a non-North Shore sort of way. They reply pretty graciously that it wasn't my fault, and I suppose it wasn't, though I do feel a bit bad about it nevertheless. And then in comes Myra, this is in the office, at work.

We giggle. 'Well, that went well.' I say. I'd invited all my students, though luckily none of them came – just the usual culture-vultures.

'So,' she asks, 'What's all this stuff about [she names the senior poet]?'

'What stuff?' I reply. 'All *I* remember is him skiting about what a hard man he still is.'

'I've just been hearing that those friends of yours told the cops that he'd been molesting young girls, including a Czech girl at the uni who complained about him.'

At this I remember an earlier part of the evening, just after the senior poet had started to read, when a voice outside the hall (obviously Donald's) had shouted something about 'fondling the buttocks of young girls.' I assumed at the time that it was just him being drunk and disorderly, as in the days when he used to write abusive letters to people, the editor of *Poetry NZ* most prominent among them.

⁂

There was something revelatory about the taste of this bookish young pharmacist … who clearly and inarguably preferred minor works to major ones. He chose *The Metamorphosis* over *The Trial*, he chose *Bartleby* over *Moby-Dick* … and *A Christmas Carol* over … *The Pickwick Papers*. What a sad Paradox, thought Amalfitano. Now even bookish pharmacists are afraid to take on the great, imperfect, torrential works, books that blaze paths into the unknown. They choose the perfect exercises of the great masters. Or what amounts to the same thing: they want to watch the great masters spar, but they have no interest in real combat, when the great masters struggle against that something, that something that terrifies us all, that something that cows us and spurs us on, amid blood and mortal wounds and stench.

– Roberto Bolaño, 2666

⚉

The cops, Myra continues, had seemed quite concerned about it – as if nowadays no such accusation can be dismissed readily as baseless for fear of later repercussions.

So it begins to look as if, rather than simply getting a bit the worse for wear and being thrown out of a venue, as happens to some of our mutual friends most nights of their lives, Donald actually *came* to Northcote with the intention of confronting the senior poet.

Kind of sickens you a bit with the 'literary life,' though, doesn't it? The voice of a writer droning on about the imaginary dilemmas of her alcoholic character, while a real alcoholic character, which is what I'm beginning to fear Donald may be, is brawling and disintegrating under all of our noses.

And yet, though it seems rather unlikely when I read over the dreary chronicle of events, there *was* something irresistibly amusing about the whole thing: the senior poet's complete and utter glee at having proved himself in combat in defence of his lady. 'You missed all the excitement!' as he shouted to Myra when she came sidling up; the looks on the faces of some of the Northcote ladies – poets unfettered just a bit too close for comfort; Hilda picking up the gossip a mile a minute.

No-one was hurt and nothing got damaged. Funnily enough, far more glasses were broken by people knocking them over with their elbows than the one destroyed by Donald, but I do feel bad for the organisers and the gallery-owners. They put a lot of work into the whole thing.

Most of the poetry that was read was, predictably, dreadful, but that's not a mortal sin either.

Tell me if you'd like to hear more of this sort of thing, or if you're relieved not to *have* to hear about the mad antics of your writerly friends. I just thought it might amuse you, but now that I look at it I guess it's not all that funny after all.

It's certainly a reading that will go down in North Shore history, though.

Lots of love from

Jack

Company

Things have been closing down around here for a while now. First it was the bank, then the post office. Next, I suppose, it'll be the supermarket. After that we'll just be left with a dairy and a petrol station. If that.

The one which really made an impact on me was the video store. I can get on a bus and cruise over to the next suburb if I want to do some banking or pay my bills. Returning an overnight DVD that way is a little less convenient, though.

The day of the great closing down sale was quite a sight to see. Everyone in town seemed to be there, though admittedly a lot of them were just kids looking for playstation games.

Us more serious types were left rummaging through the shelves of westerns and horror movies – particularly, in my case, the latter. First-run DVDs were five dollars, but everything else had been reduced to two dollars. Movement along the shelves was difficult, though, so you were pretty much confined to the first place you ended up at when the doors opened!

Why horror movies, you ask? I don't really know. They just seem to speak to me somehow. I don't watch the ones with people mutilating each other with chainsaws and hooks and chopping off each other's feet: Leatherface and Freddie Kruger and stuff like that. My preference is for the more ghostly ones, with a bit of psychology and lots of menace thrown in.

A good ghost story is hard to find, so I did have a few in mind to look for going in. Luckily it turned out that my tastes were a little bit out of the ordinary: *Lake Mungo*, *Wind Chill*, *Insidious*. I ended up with a whole armful of my favourites.

And there they sat, in a corner of my room, for quite some time after that. I knew that I should watch them to make sure they weren't scratched or otherwise damaged. If I waited too long to check, I wouldn't be able to get them cleaned up by the people in the shop, who'd said they were planning to stay open right up until Christmas.

The trouble was that I'd watched so many of them already, that it was awfully hard to sit through them again. Accordingly, I kept on putting it off till one particularly grey and rainy afternoon a week or so before Christmas.

I don't like to watch movies during the day as a general rule. The trouble with not having a regular job is that it's easy to get slack about things like that. I have to have my days all planned and plotted out to *stop* me giving into such temptations.

But, hey, what the heck, rules are made to be broken, right? I couldn't even remember half the stuff I'd got: I was shovelling them into my bag so fast I was hardly looking at them after a while.

There must have been fifty movies in that pile. A lot of them were old standards – *The Exorcist, Ring* – but surely there must be *something* there I hadn't seen.

There was, as it turned out. At some point I must have drifted over to the documentary section, since the pressure of punters was least apparent over there, because there appeared to be a number of interesting-looking 'true ghost story' DVDs in my stack as well.

There was one called *Spooked*, about an old deserted sanatorium in Kentucky, which turned out to be pretty silly: more about special effects than anything anyone had actually *seen*.

There was also an old made-for-TV film called *The Haunting*, based, allegedly, on a 'true story' about a household haunted by a demon. There was something just so matter-of-fact and circumstantial about it that I found it weirdly compelling. It was as if there was no natural arc to the story, no imposed three-act structure, which had the effect of lending it a kind of verisimilitude.

The whole thing began, I recall, with the mother of the family down in the basement. She heard someone calling out her name in what she thought was her mother-in-law's voice. On going upstairs, she found the mother-in-law denied it vehemently. She was quite upset herself. It turned out, as she subsequently admitted, that, at the same time, she'd been hearing what she thought was her daughter-in-law's voice shouting out obscenities.

And so it went on. On and on. Once, when the family were all away from home, the neighbours complained about a loud party taking place in their house. There were lights, shouting voices, crashing crockery. Nothing was out of place when they returned, however.

It went on for years: well over a decade, I think. Every twist and turn was documented in the film, and the sheer dreary intensity of it gave you something of a sense of what it must be like to be haunted yourself.

The next day, out of curiosity, I looked up the title of the film online, at the local library: nothing. There were quite a few films with titles containing variations on *The Haunting* – *An American Haunting*, *The Haunting in Connecticut*, etc. etc. This particular one had, however, left no obvious record of itself in any of the usual places: the Internet Movie Database, Wikipedia – you know the drill.

While this is, I suppose, not impossible for a made-for-TV film, the fact that it had actually made it to a video release seemed to imply that it should have left *some* traces.

I suppose that you're anticipating that when I got home I found that the disc was gone: Whoo-hoo-hoo-hoo! Spooky! No such luck. It was there, all right, with the useful appurtenances of hokey cover art and garish blurbs. There *was* a distinct absence of information about the production company, actors, date and other details one would usually expect to see – though that's not so unusual with fly-by-night companies putting out cheap materials in knock-off editions.

So I started to watch it again.

There weren't any phone calls telling me I had seven days to live, nor did any arms come out of the screen and try to pull me in. But there *was* something a little odd about the whole thing.

It's always a bit difficult to remember the exact sequence of events in a film, even one you've just seen. And while it had a main page, this disc didn't seem to have any separate list of scenes or chapters which one could use for reference. It did seem to me that not all of the things I remembered as being in the film were in it this time, though, while there were one or two sequences I didn't remember at all. One in particular, where a swinging door on a cupboard revealed a reflected face, gave me quite a nasty start. It looked so much like someone I know -- once knew, I should say.

But that's not evidence; of course it's not. You don't always watch something with your full attention: you might go wandering out of the room for a moment or two without remembering it later, so these extra bits and pieces didn't perturb me too much.

It was the absences that concerned me most. It's one thing not to notice things in a film: it's quite another to remember scenes that simply don't seem to be there anymore.

Descartes was right: one must have method. He also said that the silence of infinite spaces frightened him – or was that Pascal? I think, therefore I am.

There were chapter numbers on the video display, even though there wasn't a separate page listing the scenes. So I made my own breakdown of each of the film's sections: there were seventeen in all, counting the title and the credits.

Skipping from one to the next, timing them, adding them up, gave me a most satisfactory feeling of *control*. How can anything random enter into this mechanised universe of the video display? No, the video was purely and simply a puppet: the only wild card in the deck could be my own perceptions of what I'd seen.

And so matters rested. For a while.

⁂

I do have friends. Just not a lot of them, that's all. And a number of them have moved away over the years.

It *is* a bit harder to find people to talk to when you get to my age, though, and as for inviting them round to the house, well, people who know that you're a bachelor and you live alone tend to expect that your housekeeping is going to be a bit on the sketchy side.

I wanted to show the movie to *someone*, just to see if they saw the same things I did, if you understand what I mean. So I invited this young guy I'd talked to in the library a few times, one of the librarians, to drop round for a drink.

He was an intensely enthusiastic guy: always congratulating me on my choice of books and films to watch, the library rents those, too, so it hadn't been hard to get him into conversation – more the other way round, in fact.

That was the main burden of his remarks when he did finally turn up at the house, in fact: the difficulty of finding people to talk to when you've just moved to a new town. I had to agree with him there, though in my case that still applies despite the fact that I was born and brought up here.

He wasn't, he told me, a great fan of horror movies, being more bio-pics and other more 'educational' stuff like that.

'It's not that I mind being scared,' he confided. 'Just that I'd rather stick to what's *real*, y'understand?'

I did understand. The movie I was proposing to show him had *both* things going for it, I claimed, somewhat mendaciously. As well as being a pretty frightening story, it also had the virtue of being true.

'Really? I mean, I hadn't really meant to stay.'

'Oh, come on! Look, I've got beer; I've got potato chips. It's not that long a film! Come on, live a little.'

'All *right!*'

Talking to him was a little like entering the mind of a California surfer. The long and the short of it was that he agreed to stay.

And so I put it on again. The move to the new house; unpacking; the voice in the basement; the misunderstanding with the mother-in-law; the visit from the psychic who saw all the ghosts in the house, including the 'dark one' she couldn't properly make out, the one who was manipulating all the others, the one she thought was a demon.

I must have watched it three or four times by then, and every time I kept notes on the exact sequence of events, the material included in each numbered section of video. I'd found that once I wrote them down, they had a tendency to stay put, a conclusion very satisfying to my Cartesian sense of logic, of the impossibility of *bridging* the soul-body divide.

This time was no exception. All was as I remembered it. Everything came on cue, as the numbers unfolded on the DVD display. Quite a relief, really. I must have been a bit tired the first couple of times I watched it. There was, in fact, no other explanation.

He seemed strangely subdued after the screening, insisting on getting his coat and preparing to go even as the final credits were rolling. No 'one more for the road,' no light banter, just off into the rain, with some perfunctory thanks for the chips and the beer.

I thought nothing of it. It was kind of late by then, after all, and, while the incidents were now as familiar to me as events from my own life, I could understand someone else finding them a bit upsetting.

He seemed to avoid me after that. Even when I went up to get books issued from the counter, his conversation was most perfunctory, not at all the ready banter I'd become accustomed to from him.

Again, I thought nothing much of it. Perhaps he'd thought I was planning to make a move on him, perhaps he'd even *wanted* me to? Who can say? If you're a bachelor who lives alone, whether by choice or happenstance, you get used to the fact that just about nothing you do can be regarded as unsuspicious.

But then I noticed that the other library assistants, mostly young women, some still at High School, had started to whisper among themselves when I came in, hushing when I came near, then starting up as soon as I was out of earshot. Had he told them something about me? If so, what? What exactly was *wrong* with watching a video and drinking a beer with a new acquaintance?

I honestly couldn't think of anything I'd done to merit such suspicious and hostile glances. But then, I guess that's the problem with living alone: just because you're paranoid doesn't mean that they're not all out to get you.

I got a bit sick of it after a while, and lay in wait for him at the end of his shift.

I came up to him while he was undoing the chain on his bike, bike-clips already attached round his ankles.

'Hi there. Long time no see.'

'Oh, hi! Look, I'm in a bit of …'

'A hurry? I know. I feel as if we haven't talked since you came over that time. I've been meaning to ask you how you liked the movie?'

'The movie? Oh yeah. Well, not too much, actually. Look, I have to …'

'I know, I know, you've got to go. It's just – I feel like you've been kind of avoiding me since that night, and I just wanted to know why? I mean, was it something I said?'

'No, no, nothing like that. I've just been kind of busy. You know.'

'Yeah, I know.'

'It's just that. Look, don't take this the wrong way, but, I just don't feel that comfortable talking to you now, after …'

'After what? After I invited you over to watch a movie?'

'That's just it. After you invited me over to …'

'But what's wrong with that? I mean, if you didn't like the movie you only had to say something.'

'Didn't – like – the – movie …'

'Yeah. What was wrong with it? I mean, I know it's no blockbuster, low production values, made-for-TV.'

'Try *no* production values.'

'That's a bit *harsh*.'

'Look, I don't want to talk about it anymore. And I'd thank you not to try and speak to me again.'

'How do you mean? Stop coming to the library?'

'No, I don't suppose I can ask you to do *that*, but you don't have to come up to me when you do.'

'But what did I do? Was it something *in* the movie? I've noticed it isn't always the same every time.'

He stared at me, incredulous. 'There was no movie.'

'What do you mean there *was* no movie?'

'I mean just that. You put on the disc, and then we just sat there, in the dark, watching nothing but a blank screen.'

'Oh come *on*. If you couldn't see anything at all, why didn't you say something?'

'Say *what*? What do you say when someone puts on a film, and starts talking about the scenes, and what's going down in *this* bit and *that* bit, and you can't see anything at all? What do you say? At first I thought it must be some kind of art film, a whole lot of blankness people can see what they want to in. Then I started to wonder if there was something wrong with my eyes. It wasn't a blue screen, you understand: nor was it completely dark. Once or twice I felt that I saw a kind of a swirling motion in it, but maybe that was just the result of sitting there for so long.'

'But … I could see …'

'I know what *you* could see in it. You kept on saying. There were ghosts, family arguments, all sorts of stuff. But none of that was there. Not for me, anyway.'

'So you think I'm crazy.'

'Well, duh! At the very least I'd say you need help. But it ain't going to be me that provides it.'

And with that he wobbled off, his crash helmet still hanging from one hand, and his bag in the other. I didn't call out after him.

🀙

This afternoon I thought I'd get round to clearing out the basement of a lot of useless stuff I've been storing down there. Some of it was old books and furniture belonging to my parents, but there were still a few boxes of clothes and crockery belonging to my ex that I've been meaning to send to her. I don't have her new address, but I imagine I can send it care of her family.

While I was down there I heard a voice calling out to me.

It *sounded* like her, anyway.

When I climbed back up the stairs there was nobody there. It's a shame, really. In some ways I could do with the company.

Still, better luck next time.

General Grant in Paeroa

I met a girl from Paeroa once. It was in Tahiti, where I was living with a family on a student exchange. She didn't like me.

She didn't like me to a quite extravagant extent. I must have said something the first time we met which gave her the impression that I was a snobby Aucklander from the Eastern suburbs, looking down on the poor provincial hayseeds.

Nothing could have been further from the truth, but you know how it is once someone takes a dislike to you? Everything you say from then on somehow conspires to back up their original idea. No matter how hard you try to repair it, the damage has already been done.

Anyway, the reason I mention it here is because there is a popular soft drink here in New Zealand called 'Lemon & Paeroa.' It's a kind of lemonade made, originally, at least, with carbonated water from the local spring. It's now been bought by the Coca-Cola company, and is bottled elsewhere.

For a long time there was a rather funny TV ad campaign listing things which were 'world-famous in New Zealand', concluding with a silent pan across the huge plaster L & P bottle standing at the gateway to Paeroa.

In an unfortunate moment, when some French kids asked me to describe the town, I referred to it as the 'drinking capital of New Zealand.' By which I meant, I swear, Lemon & Paeroa. Overhearing this, though, the girl, whose name escapes me, thought – not unreasonably, I suppose – that I was describing people from Paeroa as a bunch of drunks.

Nothing I said to dispute this interpretation of my innocently meant remark had any effect. I had insulted her native soil, and was therefore the worst kind of arrogant big city aggressor.

Paeroa has done quite a bit to jazz up its Wild West image since then. For a while it made a concerted attempt to market itself as the Antiques capital of New Zealand, perhaps because the L & P label was getting a little tired. The main street filled up with shops selling bric-à-brac of various types, and the whole thing went with a bang, at first.

But Paeroa is quite a long way from anywhere else, and there are antique shops in other towns, too, and it's difficult to restock often enough to attract return custom after a day of junk-shopping there, and this was pretty high-priced junk, too. So one by one, over the years, they've folded, until now there are only a few left of the original squadron of shops offering ceramics, fabric, furniture: and scruffy books.

The second-hand bookshops were probably the first to go. On my last visit there, only about half of those I remembered still seemed to be in business. I did pick up one or two little trifles, though, including a hardback copy of Bruce Catton's American civil war book *Grant Takes Command*.

I actually walked out of the shop without it, then, half an hour later, had to trace my footsteps back. I put it back in the shelves after seeing how assiduously, almost fanatically, it had been underlined and annotated by its previous owner. It was an ex-library book, from Remuera, probably the snobbiest quarter of

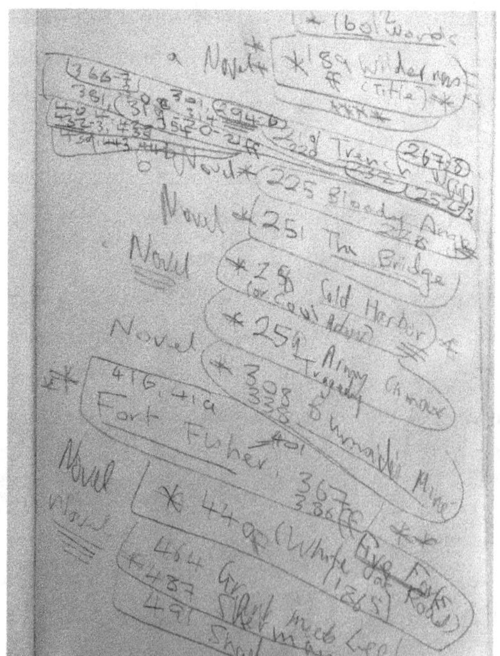

snobby Auckland, and had extensive pencil markings on virtually every page.

A book in the hand is worth two in the bush, however, so, on maturer reflection, I decided to pay the couple of dollars they were charging for it.

It was hard for me to imagine that there would be much there that was new, given that I'd already pored over the accounts of General Ulysses S. Grant's Wilderness campaign in Catton's trilogy of books about the Army of the

Potomac, not to mention his magisterial Centenary History of the Civil War. Nevertheless, when I got home I started to leaf idly through it.

You know, I'm rather glad I did.

It's a pretty ugly book. Of the cover illustration, by a certain 'Edward Mortelmans' (sounds like a pun on 'mortal man,' doesn't it?) the less said the better: Blue & Grey kitsch, concocted for the UK edition of a very American book.

The fly-leaf is distinctly more interesting, though: the list of annotations seems to imply some system to the scribbles and underlinings its former owner had undertaken so assiduously:

There are already odd features to be noted. Why, for instance, does he circle and tick the dedication of Catton's original book? Has he found out who this 'David' is? Or is there a David in his own life whom he would like to commemorate similarly?

Somehow I assumed from the beginning that this annotator was a man, though there's no direct evidence of it. Perhaps we should call him David, in fact, this anonymous commentator on Catton's work. I thought at first that it might be the first name of Bruce Catton's son, who collaborated with him on his 1963 book *Two Roads to Sumter*, but no, that was *William* Catton.

Moving on to the Table of Contents:

There it is, unequivocally, written in cold print, in capital letters, no less: 'MY NOVEL.' Or should it read 'MY NOVEL starts here'? Three chapter titles are circled: 'In the Wilderness,' 'Beyond the

Contents

Bloody Angle,' Roll On, Like a Wave' and then the final words, 'Strange Land' of the final chapter, 'Stranger in a Strange Land.'

The novel, then, seems to have been intended to cover the period from the two-day Battle of the Wilderness, through Spottsylvania and Cold Harbor, to the end of the War.

There's an interesting admission on p. 282 of the text. The 'night of June 13' (l. 10 from the top) and 'following morning, June 14' (l. 3 from the bottom) are circled, and the words '150 years ago' written at the foot of the page.

150 years added on to 1864 takes us to June 2014. Since I purchased the book in Paeroa on the 9th of January, 2015, this means that sometime in the six months intervening our prospective novelist

ipe, and said. "If we have nothing worse than this . . ." He left the sentence unfinished, and returned to his blanket. Rawlins that night wrote to Mrs. Rawlins, assuring her: "From the commencement of his campaign General Grant has not deviated at all from his written plan, but has steadily pursued the line he then marked out." [20]
On the following morning, June 14, Grant rode down to the ames. The engineer troops were hard at work, building a causeway cross low ground to the water's edge, putting more than a hundred

150 years ago [282]

must have lost faith in his project, bundled up his carefully annotated text, and consigned it to a junkshop.

That's one theory, at least.

Perhaps the book was stolen. Perhaps he died, and it was the executors of his estate who boxed it up for resale to the highest bidder. Perhaps he actually finished writing the novel he was planning, and thus felt no further need for the research materials so painstakingly gathered along the way.

That last seems unlikely to me, though. I may be more of a packrat than most, but I can't conceive of disposing of so detailed and important a source just six months after the collection of data for his projected civil war novel had begun. I'm sorry to say it, but a loss of faith in the project, or confidence in his own ability to carry it out still seems the most likely scenario.

It's not just the 150-year anniversary that appears to have obsessed him, though. Go forward 50 years from 1864, and you arrive at 1914. The 'pattern of trench warfare' referred to in Catton's account of the siege of Petersburg inevitably recall the trenches 'of WWI.'

Not only that, but if we were to take another fifty-year leap, that would take us to the middle of the1960s, the period of composition of Catton's book.

> in Virginia were concerned, the time of long marches and massive pitched battles was over. The Army of Northern Virginia would never again see northern Virginia, nor would the Army of the Potomac see the Potomac again. They were fixed in position, almost totally immobilized, and henceforth for month after dreary month they would see little more than the desolate trenches, the heavy forts that were built at every weak point, setting the pattern of trench warfare with its eternal round of shelling and sharpshooting and day-by-day discomfort of heat and dust and thirst, with its occasional furious small fights for small advantages. Richmond was a good many miles away, and yet in reality the entire layout of works was the defense of Richmond — a twenty-five-mile set of trenches and forts that began up near White Oak Swamp, east of Richmond, came down across the

There are a number of isolated passages marked with the word 'novel' – to be extracted or otherwise drawn upon, presumably, for our annotator's projected acts of imaginative recreation:

> And there it was. Grant could not make a routine military appointment without reflecting on the presidential election; indeed, the political tide was so strong and so confusing that routine military acts all became extraordinary, as if something great had to be fought out in men's minds before anyone could act on the battlefield.
>
> A peace movement was going on, and General Meade remarked that "the camp is full of rumors and reports of many kinds" as a result. The movement was largely the creation of Horace Greeley, the hard-war abolitionist editor of the New York *Tribune*, who occasionally carried a pundit's eccentricity to excess and who now had gone off on a tangent. Greeley somehow had got in touch with Confederate agents in Canada and had absorbed the idea that Lincoln could end the war if he would just sit down and talk reasonably with reasonable Confederates about a peace that would be honorable and satisfying to both sides. Greeley wrote despairingly to Lincoln about "our bleeding, bankrupt, almost dying country," he failed to realize that the only peace Richmond wanted was one that saved both Southern independence and Southern slavery . . . and unfortunately he did not know that the Confederates in Canada had no authorization to talk to Lincoln about anything. Lincoln called his bluff, giving Greeley full power to bring the supposed Confederate emissaries to the White House; Greeley finally learned that he had been talking to the wrong people and went away sorrowing, aware that he had been had and

Real, concrete clues as to the nature of the actual nature of the narrative are few and far between, however. We have a number of suggested titles – 'The Horseman':

along the way from the James river up to Gettysburg" — that is, in the army's story in the days before Grant — and although the soldiers did have prejudices they were solidly loyal to the Union, "however blind they may have been to the personal identity of 'that Western man' with the cause for which they fought." [17]
    Grant and Lincoln shared something, here. They were westerners, lacking in polish, unable to impress the cultivated easterners. Early in the war Lincoln's minister to Great Britain, Charles Francis Adams,

'That Western Man':

Roughshod or On Tiptoe

To sit unconcerned on a log, away from the battlefield whittling — to be a man on horseback or smoking a cigar — seems to exhaust the admiration of the country; and if this is really just, then Nero fiddling over burning Rome is sublime."
    The feeling of a certain part of the officer corps was summed up by Lieutenant Colonel Carswell McClellan, who had served on General

not to mention 'A Good Loyal Man,' all of which might lead us to expect that he meant to write an account focussing on General Grant himself. Perhaps a first-person narrative, even? A little like Richard Adams' book *Traveller* (1988), where Robert E. Lee's horse narrates the tale of his role in the Lost Cause in cod Southern dialect?

The existence of Grant's own much-praised autobiographical account of the war, completed in the hope of retrieving his family's blasted fortunes under the shadow of his last heroic fight with cancer, might lead one to see that last plan as somewhat supererogatory, however.

A great deal of underlining has been applied to the very last pages of Catton's book, where he tries to sum up the effect of the war on those who had fought in it:

One of Sherman's veterans, going home with all the rest, found that when the armies did melt back into the heart of the people the adjustment was a little difficult. The men had been everywhere and had seen everything. Life's greatest experience had ended with most of life still to be lived, to find a common purpose in the quiet days of peace would be hard: 'Old avenues are closed to them, old ambitions are dead, and they walk as in a dream – as strangers in a strange land.'

This latter quote is attributed by Catton to F. Y. Hedley's 1890 memoir *Marching Through Georgia* (p. 488). The underlying reference is, though, of course, to the Bible: 'I have been a stranger in a strange land' [Exodus 2: 22]. As Catton goes on to say: 'One of these veterans moving along a shadowed new path after living in a world where he had seen the path so very clearly, was General Grant.'

So what did happen to 'MY NOVEL' and the bright hopes that motivated so energetic a ransacking of volume three of this biography of General U. S. Grant?

It is, alas, impossible to say -- on the evidence I have, at any rate. For all I know 'The Horseman' is with a publisher right now, being readied for the Christmas trade. After all, this may be only one of many tomes our anonymous author pored over whilst creating his great work.

Later That Summer is the title of the imaginary civil war novel composed by one of the offstage characters in Stephen King's rather aptly-titled 1994 novel *Insomnia*. It was supposed to be an account of what happened to Robert E. Lee's Army of Northern Virginia after their defeat at the Battle of Gettysburg, and was clearly envisaged as a kind of sequel to Michael Shaara's classic *The Killer Angels* (1974), later dramatised (exceptionally poorly), as the four-hour movie epic *Gettysburg* (1993).

The omni-talented Australian writer Thomas Keneally has also written a civil war novel: *The Confederates* (1979), about Lee's first, and equally unsuccessful, invasion of the North, culminating in the Battle of Antietam, or – if you prefer – Sharpsburg.

So there's nothing inherently improbable or absurd about writing a novel based on the last days of Grant's campaign in Virginia. Shelby Foote, even, the great Shelby Foote, wrote the single-battle-focussed novel *Shiloh* (1952) before embarking on his great Homeric trilogy about the civil war.

I may be wrong – very probably am, in fact – but I can't help wondering if it was the consummate showmanship of Tony Award winner Tony Kushner's script for the Steven Spielberg film *Lincoln* (2012), not released here till 2013, which put our prospective author off?

There does seem to be a suspicious amount of coincidence with the focus of some of the anonymous underlinings in the Catton book: the emphasis on the Confederate peace mission in the first days of 1865 is common to both, as are many other details. After all, he may not have seen it when it first came out. Perhaps he downloaded or rented it sometime in late 2014, and felt that he'd been gazumped.

Whatever the explanation for his abandonment of the project, or at any rate Bruce Catton's book, I sometimes feel that I'd like to pick up where he left off – re-enter the Gothic dreamscapes of *Cold Mountain*, *The Beguiled* and all those other civil war classics – and write my own tale of Grant's murderous advance on Richmond in the late Spring and Summer of 1864. It would be a kind of homage to a fellow-worker in the field of fiction, however serious his intentions actually were.

I can't help feeling, though, that it might be taken amiss: outside appropriation of something better left to natives, another innocent remark about L & P which might come across as dismissive or patronising.

Better, perhaps, to dream of another kind of novel, based on a quite different classic of historical writing, James Cowan's 2-volume *The New Zealand Wars* (1922), fleshed out by his firsthand interviews with the survivors of our own land wars of the 1840s and 1860s.

Paeroa began as a gold-mining town, built in 1875, long after the wars, on land bought from two local Māori Chiefs, Tukukino and Taraia. Nor was the surrounding region particularly associated with the fighting, being too far east for the Waikato war and too far north for the campaigns of the great warrior prophet Te Kooti Arikirangi Te Turuki in the late 1860s.

There is, however, one intriguing reference to Paeroa in *Papers Past*, the online repository of so much nineteenth-century pioneer journalism. It comes from the *New Zealand Herald* for 29 June 1883:

TE KOOTI AT PAEROA, OHINEMURI

I am informed that Te Kooti, and about fifty followers, have visited
Paeroa, and besides being the 'lions' of the place were masters of
the situation. They were impartial patrons of the hotels. A guard
was mounted at each, and none of the rank and file were allowed
more than a pint of beer. Not so, the doughty chief, his rangatiras,
and his secretary. They fraternised with a deputations [sic.] of
'illustrious' citizens, and champagne and brandy were quaffed
right heartily, and of course friendship pledged. As far as concerns
the publicans, the most interesting feature to them will be, who is
to pay for the liquor consumed? It was deemed not only proper but
essential that due deference should be paid to 'the man of blood.'
The well-known surveyor, (Mr R. C. Long) was smoking his pipe
when the secretary intimated that he must cease to do so in the
presence of Te Kooti. Mr. Long promptly complied, but whether
as a mark of respect or esteem or an act of discretion, the public
have not yet been enlightened.

Te Kooti was pardoned by the government in 1883, shortly before this visit,
but was subsequently imprisoned when he attempted to revisit his old home
in the East of the North Island. He was released on the understanding that he
should not try to return to his old haunts, a decision upheld by the Court of
Appeal in 1890. By then it was clear that he was an incurable alcoholic. He died
a couple of years later.

The rather facetious tone the *Herald*'s Thames correspondent uses about this
'man of blood,' a phrase last used, if I'm not mistaken, for King Charles the
First in the English Civil Wars, is typical of late nineteenth-century European
attitudes to Māori. No-one was laughing in 1868, when Te Kooti and his men
slaughtered fifty four settlers at Matawhero, in response, it is thought, to his
unjust imprisonment on the Chatham Islands.

General Grant, too, ended badly. His tour of the world at the conclusion of
his second term as president took him to New Zealand in 1879, where he too,
alas, displayed 'intemperance' at a state banquet, and was even accused by a local
newspaperman of ogling some of the young girls present with inappropriate
zeal.

Perhaps one could contrive some kind of meeting? Te Kooti's favourite mode of transportation was on a white charger, and Grant, too, was immensely fond of horses. Could they have met out riding, somewhere in the Hauraki Plains, and shared a libation from Grant's hipflask? Why not, after all?

Whichever way one plays it, though, it's a pretty sad story: Grant's solitary last days out on the veranda, labouring away at his memoirs, as penniless and disgraced as he was when the Civil War began. Te Kooti, expelled by the Māori King from the great 1878 peace conference at Hikurangi for breaking the ban on alcohol, reduced to cadging drinks from strangers in the hotels of Paeroa. 'David,' our putative author, starting his civil war novel with such high hopes, then discarding the sedulously annotated ex-library book which had inspired it all in a Hospice shop a few short months later.

Let's honour them all, obscure and famous, rich and poor, invader and native. Conflict brings strange bedfellows. 'It is well,' to quote the great Virginian Robert E. Lee, 'that war is so terrible – we would grow too fond of it!'

Brothers

We've tried phone calls – but they always end up in shouting, somehow.

We've tried email – but he said that he'd grown so to dread the 'cold aggression' of my tone that he could hardly bring himself to open my messages anymore.

We've tried skype – but I found I couldn't bear staring directly into his beady little eyes for so long a time.

Face to face actually works best, but only because I can usually position myself so that I don't have to look at him, and can thus constantly retreat into other, more pleasant regions of thought.

And yet we *must* talk, for a while longer, at least. Family business demands it, and no further evasions can be found.

And along with that, of course, comes a raft of other family obligations, Birthday and Christmas cards, presents, even, however token in nature. All those enforced contacts which gall us most when they seem most arbitrary.

So what to get him for Christmas?

A copy of Emily Post, was my first thought, though it turned out, when I mentioned this jest to someone at work, that no-one appears to recall anymore her undisputed reign over all the intricacies of etiquette.

A film? I've tried that before, buying the alleged Sinophile a box-set of Chinese historical epics. But his look of complete incomprehension at the gift persuaded me that this was not an expedient worth repeating.

A book, then? The fact that the books are piled high in his house thick as autumnal leaves that strew the brooks in Vallombrosa might suggest otherwise. Still, where best to hide a leaf? In the forest. What best to buy for a misanthrope? More of what he already has.

A book was accordingly determined on. But what book? Nothing about self-help, that's for sure: too pointed. There's no need to escalate the temperature when it's already at boiling point.

I'd watched a particularly nasty ghost story sometime before: about a vengeful spirit who rejects all attempts to appease her, and instead ends up killing her would-be benefactor.

I'd seen the book it was based on some weeks before, bound up with several other stories by the same hand, in a little bookshop some half an hour away by car.

Having left it so late, the holiday frenzy was already in full spate when I decided to drive over and get it. Crowds were thronging the malls, aggressive motorists the roads. It was fearfully hot, sweatily, stickily hot, and the busdrivers were on strike.

Nevertheless, I duly set out on my fool's errand, to buy something avowedly useless for someone I don't like in order to try to persuade him that I *do* – when all the time he and I both know that all of this is just about the money, a great deal of money, which neither of us wishes to dissipate in lawyer's fees so long as there's any chance at all of getting our share by simply watching and waiting, Hallelujah! Deck the halls with boughs of holly, and fa la la la la la la la la, give or take a 'la' or two.

It used to be that the fastest way to drive across town was to avoid all the suburban capillary roads by getting straight onto the motorway. No longer, alas.

It took me so long even to get onto the motorway *approach* the last time I tried it that I've taken to putting up with all the fifty kilometre speed limits and random old ladies out in their little blue cars in the interests of simply keeping moving, and thus discouraging my sad antique of a car from overheating.

And there's no denying that it's more interesting inching one's way through a built-up shopping centre than one more random stretch of soulless highway.

Which is why, I suppose, I had the leisure to see the ghost.

I say 'ghost,' but that is, of course, a supposition. How am I to confirm that it was a ghost, and not a hallucination, or even just a trick of the light in my eyes?

The fact remains that I saw, by the side of the road, my ex-wife standing, parcels in hand, waiting for the pedestrian crossing lights to go green.

Methought I saw my late espousèd Saint, etc. etc. Not *Saint*, though, never that – but not a face, or a frown, I could ever grow indifferent to, either, no matter how much time had gone by.

And she was frowning, that was the thing: despite all the Christmas trappings around her, all the green trees and red hats and bundles of presents, all those things she most loved, she had that crease in her forehead which denoted distress.

There was nowhere to stop. I suppose I could have abandoned the car and leapt out and run back to accost her, but it was not – in the mundane sense, at least – a feasible manoeuvre. But I could hardly just drive on, either, so I turned down a side-street and came back, by a commodious vicus of circulation, to the same intersection.

Where she was, of course, no longer standing.

Had she ever been there at all? Well, I suppose that it depends in what sense you mean the question. Would she have been visible to anyone else seated beside me? Possibly not. But that doesn't mean that she hadn't been clearly apparent to *me*, despite the fact that I wasn't thinking about her, and hadn't, in fact, spent a moment on her for what seemed like years.

I ranged around the shopping centre for a while, having finally found a park in the nearby mall, but with little result, and nothing to show for it besides perplexity.

Could it have been her? There was no real reason why not. Despite the fact that she lived on the other side of the world, in the approximate zone of the white Christmas, she *could* have made a sudden decision to revisit old haunts at the season of goodwill. Why not, in fact?

I hadn't heard anything from her, was one reason why not, but then she did have some fairly distant relatives here. Perhaps she was visiting them? There was certainly nothing unbelievable in the idea that she wouldn't trouble herself to make contact with one whom she had somewhat unceremoniously dumped so many years before.

Who knows? The heart, any faint vestiges of heart, had gone out of my errand, but that didn't seem a strong enough reason to give up on it entirely. In the absence of alternate directions, let inertia carry you in the same trajectory, is the usual rule in these matters. And so I went on.

Backing and filling my way out of the parking building was quite adventurous enough, but given that all that had to be done anyway whether I turned left, towards the bookshop, or right, towards home, I let the ease of the leftward drift carry me on.

Till I saw her dog.

It was a big Briard sheepdog, black as night, called Ajax. I'd never exactly got on with the dog, but we'd maintained mutually respectful relations during most of the time I'd been married. With *her*, on the other hand, and the rest of the extended family, he'd been on the most rapturously loving terms.

There he was, standing by the side of the road, staring fixedly into space, as if at some imaginary point in the distance. I remembered his uncanny skill at detecting where a car was going whilst still some minutes or miles away from the destination: with intense excitement if it was to see one of his loved ones, dejection if it was merely to the vet or the grooming clinic.

He certainly wasn't looking at *me*, and, so far as I could ascertain in the brief glimpse I got of the other side of the road whilst driving by, nor was his mistress anywhere in sight.

I've read *Phantasms of the Living*. I know that most sightings of people who couldn't possibly be there in the flesh are not at the point of their death, or at the moment they're on the operating table, or in the grip of some extreme emotion. It can correspond with *nothing significant at all* − for either the perceiver or the thing perceived.

I also know about fetches: those strange visitations of totem animals or uncanny sights which betoken some ill luck to the beholder. Gunnar's vision of a hillside covered with blood at the climax of *Njal's Saga*, for instance.

What, then, was *this*? An omen or a happenstance? A meaningful intervention from the paranormal realm, or a mere coincidence?

On I drove, towards the bookshop, towards Susan Hill's *The Woman in Black and Other Ghost Stories*, towards my destiny, towards the distinct possibility that my brother would get his way, and all those weighty wads of dosh, to keep as company for himself alone as the night falls and the darkness comes *wherein all the beasts of the forest do move*.

Catfish

Last night, before I went to bed, I opened the curtains and looked outside.

I can't remember exactly why: to stare at the moon, perhaps.

This morning, when I woke up, the curtains were closed again. Who did that? Was it the wind, as Tanya said? She's the neighbour who comes in once a week to clean. It doesn't seem very likely to me. But if not, then *who*?

Drawn curtains are just a small thing: possible evidence of some agency at work. But the real coincidence was with my evening's viewing. I've got into the habit of watching a reality show called *American Pickers*, about a couple of unkempt bozos from Iowa who drive around in a van 'picking' through old attics and outbuildings and barns for various types of antiques, mostly car or petrol-related.

The episode I watched last night included a discussion between the two of them where Frank said he'd drawn back the curtains in the night to check on the van out in the parking lot, only to find them closed again in the morning. Mike asked him if he believed in ghosts, and Frank replied 'yes'.

That's the point I'd like to stress – the fact that he said *yes*. The detail of the curtains is suggestive, almost as if the thing in the house were listening. It *was*, if it's really me, or some level of me. But Mike's leap to talking of ghosts was significant. It shows how inevitable that corollary is, *has* to be, really. Connections.

☬

I suppose it's a bit sad that this notebook has turned out to be almost exclusively a record of my reading and viewing. It's not that I don't talk to people: I talk to Tanya whenever she comes over, for instance. Our weekly cup of tea together has become a definite ritual now.

It's just that most of my imaginative life is now conducted in the third person, in communication with the writers of books and the creators, for the most part, of bad TV. Sometimes when I hear myself reacting with mutters and groans to what the people on the screen are saying. Does that mean that things have already gone too far?

I suppose that that's what comes of moving house so soon after a death. It's not that I had a real choice in the matter: the lease on our flat did not belong to me, but to my wife, part of her inheritance from her own parents. And moving here did seem to make sense at the time: beach, open air, shops, the kind of little enclave retirees all claim to like. It's just so *boring*, though.

Except for those little things: the toothbrush in the middle of the bathroom floor this morning, the creaks and groans upstairs in the night. Those are the reverse of boring, really. Or perhaps it can feel dull even to be scared sometimes.

⚶

There's no dialogue at all in the first half hour of *The Quiet Earth*. Most people wouldn't notice that unless they, like me, had listened to the director's commentary on the film, included in the special edition of the DVD.

It makes sense, though, a film about an empty world, with a single protagonist, good old Bruno Laurence, the first real Kiwi movie-star, moving through the featureless landscape between Coromandel and Auckland – what is there to say? And to whom?

It was only after many repeat viewings that I began to pick up on the patterns. And I'm not talking Minotaur posters on the wall, or German names for typewriters, either. The test of a good theory *has* to be that it's apparent to others once you've pointed it out. Most of the ways people have found to interpret such works as Kubrick's *The Shining* founder on that simple principle.

I've been trying to write an article about it. I don't know why. I guess because that *was* my stock in trade: the high demotic critical mode. It is, I suppose, my version of a writerly comfort zone.

Here's what I have so far:

The first fruits of this new dispensation in New Zealand fiction can be seen in Craig Harrison's 'empty world' novel *The Quiet Earth* (1981). His protagonist, John Hobson ('Zac' in Geoff Murphy's 1985 film) wakes up in a world from which the rest of humanity has mysteriously disappeared.

Hobson's phantasmagoric odyssey from Thames to Wellington takes him through the very heartland of provincial New Zealand realism, and straight into conflict with the 'other' – another survivor, a Māori soldier.

As the story proceeds, it becomes clearer and clearer to us how much of what Hobson sees is influenced by the experiences and paradigms inside his head: that he is, in a sense, 'creating' the events he describes.

Unlike the film, which ends with its protagonist sprawled on a beach in an alien world, where he's somehow been transported by an exploding power station, the book ends with Hobson killing himself, again.

As he wakes up in the sunlit bedroom of the Thames motel where the story began, we realise, finally, the motivation for his reluctance to pull up the blind and expose himself once more to 'the enormous light.' He has been here before. He is enacting his own misanthropic dream of a world without the pain of other people.

҈

It's not that things were that great before I moved here. You know what they say, moving to change your life founders on the fact that you tend to find yourself waiting in the new place.

Beth's illness was *absorbing*, I'll say that for it. New drugs, new treatments, frequent midnight dashes to the hospital for some complication or other. I toyed for a while with the idea of writing a memoir about that: 'My Struggle with My Wife's Terminal Illness,' but that foundered on the fact that it had to be her story to tell.

What did I really know about it, there on the outside? What was it *really* like?

I'll never know, and I'm not sure that it does much good dwelling on such things anyway.

Certainly, accepting early redundancy, there was quite a queue but they gave me precedence due to 'personal circumstances,' and transplanting here was intended to free me up for other things, Golden ager activities of all sorts. I don't like golf, or water sports, or anything much like that except for taking long walks.

I do do that, I suppose, take walks. For the rest, the folly of moving away was that it broke my ties with just about everyone: work acquaintances as well as friends. A few of them have come down to visit, but never twice.

Beth was the one for that sort of thing: the one who could make it all seem like an adventure: somehow create the illusion that anyone should actually want to make a special trip to see us. Now there's just me, and I'm forced to acknowledge, once and for all, that I *am* the boring one.

So is she the one twitching curtains, making bumping noises in the attic upstairs? It doesn't seem much like her. But perhaps she's got something to say. It's hard to know what exactly, though. Open up? Wake up and smell the coffee?

҈

I've been trying to keep going with the Craig Harrison essay. I wanted to say what it's all 'about' – the figure in his carpet, I suppose – but found myself getting more and more confused the more words I put down:

> The strength of the idea behind Harrison's novel is, however, not so much in this use of Nietzsche's 'eternal return' as a plot-structuring device, as the facility with which it enables him to discuss the racial, post-colonial themes so close to his heart.
>
> Far more effectively than in the more programmatic *Broken October*, Hobson's suspicions, fears, and final downright homicidal ferocity against Apirana Maketu – note the closeness of that surname to *mākutu* [curse] – map Pākehā paranoia with deadly accuracy.
>
> Harrison's novel is, then, not just about New Zealand, but the precision of its local setting gives it an almost mythopoeic force.

What I *wanted* to talk about was that strange beast that hunts John Hobson, as he moves down the spine of *Te Ika a Maui*, Maui's fish, the North Island of New Zealand. That's the bit that eluded the film makers, who chose instead to halt his journey halfway, in Hamilton.

He runs into it, almost literally, on the way to Rotorua:

> I had glimpsed, briefly, a bone-white beast the size of a big dog or a calf, hairless, wet and pallid like an abortion. Its head was deformed, a mutant of dog and goat, yet fat and imbecile, wide mouth snarling to the roots of its teeth, and glistening with spit; the car lights had glared back from red points of eyes rimmed pink.

Harrison does his feeling of panic and even *indignation* at the sheer unnaturalness of the sight very well, I think:

> The car ran round bends squealing and roaring. How did I miss hitting the thing? It had gone straight at my left headlight but here'd been no sound or impact. I kept staring in the rear-view mirror half expecting the abomination to be coming after me; no, nothing but dark.

He drives on to Rotorua, 'The stench was the same as ever, like shit in hell', and finds a bed on the sixth floor of a tourist hotel.

> I know what I saw back there. If it was real then there were now things living on earth which should be dead, which defied every law of nature I ever knew. And there must be a reason for that. Something I could not live with, in any sense. It demanded my death.
>
> And if what I saw had slid into my retina from inside my mind, then God help me.

ᚠ

Yesterday something happened.

It was, I suppose, Tanya's doing. It turns out that all those odd, inexplicable-seeming things: disarranged pencils, curtains knocked out of shape, do indeed have a single cause – but there's nothing supernatural about it.

She found it curled up by the rubbish bins: a mangy little stray. I've never been much for pets, really: no space for a dog in our flat in town, and while I do remember having a cat for a while when we were kids, I don't recall feeling any great attachment to it.

This bundle of fur looked half-starved when she brought it in. She decided a bowl of milk was the safest thing, and it soon started to lap away at it like a mad thing (with unfortunate consequences a short time later, it should be said).

Its markings are curiously symmetrical, considering how many bands of light and dark fur, orange and white layers it has. I was struck by the splayed, almost leonine gravitas of its paws, from which I conclude that it is most probably a male.

It was when it was sick on the floor that I began to feel something other than bemusement in the face of this invasion from the outside world, however. It looked up at me with such a guilty air, almost flinching in advance from the shouting and blows it seemed to expect, that I couldn't help wanting to comfort it, comfort *him*, that is.

I've called him 'Hobson's Choice,' rather a mouthful, I know, but I imagine he'll settle into it as 'Hob' or even 'Choice.'

Tanya prefers the former, so 'Hob' it will be.

ᚠ

The Quiet Earth is, basically, a novel about suicide. Its surface preoccupations with colonial guilt and racism, however strongly expressed, mask an obsession with the details of what might happen after death, especially if that death came out of despair.

Immediately after his terrifying encounter with the strange abortion / shadow-creature, Hobson 'put the muzzle of the shotgun in my mouth and reached down to the trigger.' On this occasion, though, 'I could do nothing.'

It isn't till long afterwards, in narrative time, after he and his companion Apirana have run down the one surviving woman in Wellington in their car, by accident, but really as a result of the macho rivalry between them, and the two of them have fought to a finish – Hobson wins, sort of – that he finally has the strength to go back to his point of origin and complete the deed.

His realization, at that point, that he hated his own autistic son and indeed caused his death by drowning, linked to the fact that he and his wife spent their honeymoon in Rotorua, gives some substance to his sense that he is indeed creating the circumstances around him: that they constitute a kind of psychological parody of the conditions of his own life.

Of course, as luck would have it, when he does finally muster the guts to kill himself, he wakes up again, in the same hotel room, with presumably the same journey of self-discovery to endure.

No wonder the film chose a more cosmic ending, with its hero knocked through a hole between worlds into beautiful alien beachscape, with a ringed, Saturn-like planet climbing up from a strangely tranquil sea.

The fact that this is clearly the same West Coast beach which he swam at earlier in the movie, might offer a hint towards the inescapable self-referential *mise-en-abîme* which lies at the heart of the book.

But why do these stories all have to end in tragedy? *A Ring of Bright Water, Midnight Express, Old Yaller* – no sooner is some endearing animal introduced, than the mechanics of narrative construction begin to plot its destruction.

Can't we all just live happily ever after?

I took Hob to the vet for his first check-up. He's not very old: maybe six weeks or a couple of months, they said. The consensus of opinion was that he might have been abandoned by someone driving through town, but no-one really knows.

Certainly he doesn't seem to be local, and no-one has reported such a kitten as lost. There's a most heart-breaking display of such flyers on the vet's notice-board, which I read through half-reluctantly, so firmly do I find myself already attached to my little visitor.

He's now been spayed, and de-wormed, and given his vaccinations. He's lying on my bed nursing his discomforts, only half-mollified with the pieces of fish I purchased on the way home. A sad little kitten is he.

🕱

Tanya's a bustling, self-important kind of woman: the kind who expects lesser beings to follow her lead.

Her kids have left home, she tells me: some two or three years since. Her partner preceded them by ten years or so. The nature and perversity of his various misdeeds form a good deal of her conversation over cups of tea.

Those cups of tea are getting more frequent, in fact. Under the pretext of 'seeing how Hob is', or 'hearing him meowing outside', she's taken to dropping by most mornings.

This is, admittedly, an interruption to my work, but given that such work consists largely, nowadays, of biting my nails and staring at the blank echoing void of the computer screen – before giving up and starting to check out the news sites – I can't say I mind particularly.

When I first took her up on her offer to come over and clean, I feared that our interactions might be awkward. I *hate* that Lord of the Manor kind of thing, giving orders, telling people what to do. But she didn't need much telling. Nor did she make any bones, right from the beginning, about brewing up some tea and sitting me down at the table to drink it with her.

I offered to go out in the mornings when she was coming over, but she pooh-poohed the idea. 'It's no trouble. Get on with what you're doing. It certainly won't bother me.'

Now, when we meet so more frequently, you might think we'd find it difficult to find enough things to talk about. But there's the kitten. He's always up to something. So are her kids. She doesn't see them often, but they do drop by, and ring up with various crises.

I haven't told her much about my life before I came here, but she knows I was a teacher of sorts. She also knows I'm 'bookish', and am always scribbling away at something or other.

In fact, the whole thing might have panned out just as she'd planned if it hadn't been for that phone-call.

'Is this the gentleman of the house?'

'It is,' I replied warily. Phonecalls from strangers seldom bear good news, as my old Gran used to say.

'Mr … [*something I didn't catch at first*]?'

'No, that's not my name,' I replied, on the verge of hanging up.

'But you're the one who bought the cat?'

'The cat?'

'Yes, the little tabby cat. This was the number we were given.'

'I *do* have a cat. But I didn't buy him. He's a stray.'

'Is there someone else there? Your wife, perhaps? She *said* it was for someone else.'

'I'm not married.'

'Oh, well, this is the number we were given. And there's some paperwork on the cat, his vaccination book, the receipt, a couple of things like that, which got left behind when she picked it up. If you'll give me your address, I can send it on. That is, I *suppose* it must be for your kitten.'

'A little tabby, with white paws and a bib, and lots of stripes?'

'I guess so. I haven't seen him myself. It's just my job to follow up on the paperwork. I don't know why the folder wasn't sent on straight away. Perhaps it was a present, some kind of surprise?'

'Look, can I ring you back. I just need to think for a bit.'

'Of course, but if you'll just give me your address, I can post them off, and …'

I put down the phone.

'What an idiot!' was my first thought. As if a small kitten would turn up by chance, right outside my doorstep, and turn out to be just the answer to my prayers!

Then I thought of getting a hammer out of the woodshed and going around to Tanya's house and bashing her head in with it. That one appealed strongly to me for quite a while, I'm ashamed to say.

She'd really fooled me, that was the thing! Lonely old widower, obviously with a bob or two, already housetrained and broken to the plough: what more could a woman want?

Then I looked down at Hob. He was purring and licking his paws. I thought of the kinds of books I read sometimes: of nailing him up outside Tanya's door with a message taped to his front – of killing him and her and me and everyone all together and setting the gas cylinder to blow up and finish us all in a blaze of glory.

He turned up his little face and smiled at me. He was so soft and warm.

Quite clever of her, I suppose. God knows I needed *something*.

The Cross-Correspondences

Lean near to life.

Lean very near – nearer.

Max Beerbohm, 'Enoch Soames'

1

I noticed her first when she came to my office to complain. Not about me, she said, but about some of the other students in the class. Some lewd jokes had been made, and she didn't feel comfortable with things like that. She was a young Chinese girl, and it must have taken considerable courage to come in and talk to her teacher about such matters. I told her I'd do my best to cut short any such remarks in future, and – I hope – persuaded her that I disapproved of them as much as she did. Which was true, or at least half-true. I *was* certainly sorry that she'd been upset by them.

2

It was a large, unruly class, spirited and hard to control. After that, I made a conscientious effort to turn the conversation away from anything that could be construed as risqué, though I'm afraid I fell short of actually having a class discussion on the matter. She seemed to feel we'd made a connection, however. A few months later, after the end of the summer break, she sent me a message asking to meet me for a cup of tea. I was wary of such encounters, having felt on the edge of impropriety once or twice in the past, but felt in this case it would be churlish to refuse.

3

We arranged to meet at a campus café. I was careful to sit in full view, at an outside table. pedagogical paranoia is a whole subject in itself, never closing the door when talking to a female student, trying to avoid any ambiguous statements in oral or written form, keeping one's paper trails active at all times. She arrived, and promptly produced a present she'd bought for me, a pair of small porcelain teacups. We chatted for a while. She'd had a hard time. Her home was in Harbin, in the North of China, reputed to be, at certain times of year, the coldest place on earth. Sure enough, she'd got sick on her return, and had had to lie in bed for a month, her face turned to the wall.

4

Just at this moment the worst possible thing in the world happened. My strategy of sitting prominently out in the open backfired. One of the other students from last semester's tutorial group happened to be walking by, and seeing me sitting and talking to one of his former classmates, assumed that it must be some kind of reunion. He immediately came over to join us. As he'd been one of the offenders who prompted the original complaint, the sheer misfortune of this is hard to exaggerate. And then some of the other students saw us! Other members of the class, who just happened to be walking by, came over to sit at the table. The conversation became more raucous. They started to chatter about car-pooling, and some of their misadventures with terrible student drivers.

5

I could see the hurt look on the Chinese girl's face. She had, as she thought, arranged a private meeting with me, had come along with a gift, and now was relegated to being just one of the people seated at the table. There was really nothing I could do, short of asking them all to go away. They would have asked why, and if I'd replied I was meeting with her by arrangement, it would have seemed most inappropriate. She was an attractive young woman, after all, and, albeit an *ex*-student, still one studying at my institution. Eventually she left, and we never spoke to each other again.

6

That look of betrayal, though: the sense of the sheer shock she must have felt from her very natural assumption that I'd gone out of my way to invite all those other students simply to gazump our 'date', will never leave me, I think. I was completely innocent of malign motives. The horrible coincidence of just those students passing at just that minute never recurred – I don't recall seeing any of them again, even – but I would quite understand if she saw me, from that moment on, as a fraud, one who'd actively connived at their mockery of her, and therefore as someone quite unworthy of her trust.

7

Chinese girl students
taking selfies
without cameras
through the perspex
bus-stop

Watching through the
the windscreen
I debate
is this the end
prepared for me?

I feel a poem
coming on
I wish it were
much better
more nuanced

more profound

8

Rotten as the Red Chamber Hotel. That was the new slogan I came up with this morning for the fleapit they've put me in. Not that it *is* a fleapit, exactly. On the surface, it's the very model of a modern luxury hotel, with serviced apartments as well as rented rooms, glittering mirror-glass, obsequious flunkies, discreet carpeting everywhere. It's only when you've been here for a little while that the cracks begin to show. The fact that it's impossible to turn the heat down inside the rooms, for instance. There's a thermostat on the wall, but it doesn't matter which direction you dial it in, conditions remain essentially the same.

9

Mind you, it's cold outside. *Very* cold, in fact. Beijing in November is not a particularly hospitable place. You do get clear days, with high, blue sky arching off into infinity. For the most part, though, there's omnipresent grey fog verging on yellow smog: on bad days, anyway. It's not so hard to imagine why they'd want to keep the heat on high inside. Not that any of this is of much help with my assignment. I am supposed to be enjoying this place, I suppose: coming up with breezy travelogues to inspire other teachers to consider Northern China as their pedogogical destination of choice. Let's ignore the surly faces in the lifts and on the streets, the game of dodgem cars they euphemistically call 'crossing the road' in these parts.

10

Let's focus on the positive, then, turn that frown upside down, keep smuggling them bananas. I mean, after all, how bad can it be: a free trip to China on the Department? I was going to say, 'all expenses paid,' but all expenses *don't* seem to be paid. The small amount of money I changed at the airport is gradually eking away, and none of my cards seem to work in the ATMs outside. Luckily the hotel insisted on taking an impression of my credit card when I arrived, and putting 1,000 Yuan on it. I've been using that up on room service, 'charge to room.' Will I be able to get any of that back when I get home? When *do* I leave for home, anyway? Though I only just got here, really. Didn't I?

11

Sorry, so sorry — back on track: Judging from what all the websites say, there are three major things one really must do here: **Visit the Forbidden City**, **Hike on Great Wall**, and **Visit parks** (Ming Tombs, Summer Palace, Beihai Park). So there's really no point in doing any more whining in this journal until those objectives have been accomplished. Certainly there seems scant prospect of going home till then. My plan is to tick them off one after the other until there's nothing any of my colleagues can say to imply that I didn't make the best of this once-in-a-lifetime opportunity, this chance to sample the riches of Earth's oldest continuous culture.

12

I like pretending to be a writer. After a while, if you've kept up the pretence successfully enough, you start to see your name listed in reference books, and even printed objects with your name on them in bookshops. At that point you start to wonder if you really *are* a writer, and, if so, what a 'writer' actually is. There was a wonderful moment in the spin-off series from Donald Trump's reality show *The Apprentice* when the new host, Martha Stewart, heard one of the aspiring candidates recite that old cliché 'fake it 'til you make it.' For some unknown reason, Martha took great exception to this. 'I've never faked anything!' she trumpeted. 'I went to *jail*, for God's sake!'

13

Since her incarceration was, as I understand it, due to a conviction for fraud and insider trading, it's hard to see why this should stand as any great proof of integrity. However, given that the other great *bon mot* from the series was the claim, by one of her interior-design underlings, that 'Martha's really into taxidermy,' it was tempting to conclude that her grasp on the difference between reality and fiction was tenuous at best. As for the 'reality' or otherwise of the claim to be a writer, I guess that in my own case I've spent so long studying the career trajectories and sufferings of various of my literary heroes and heroines – Acker, Borges, Lowell, Pessoa – that I eventually realised that one didn't need very many external markers of success to substantiate this particular life-lie. If it really *is* a lie, that is.

14

It isn't that I don't scribble insistently. If *that* constitutes writing, then I was definitely a writer from an early age. Actually forcing myself to reread and edit my own scribblings took rather longer to achieve, but even that became possible once I'd taken the leap and decided to start using the terrifying 'w'-word. Perhaps the claim to be a writer is a little like believing oneself to be a saint. In both cases, the accolade can only really be conferred from the outside. Just because you pray all the time and try to do good works means nothing in itself. You might be quite wrong in thinking that inner voice you hear is really the voice of God. There *is* such a thing as mental illness, after all.

15

How exactly are the early spiritual yearnings of the poet William Cowper to be distinguished from his later years of full-fledged religious mania? Because he was allowed to remain at large at first, and subsequently locked up? The question remains an open one. There are certain complications surrounding 'coming out' as a writer in a country as small as my own. For a start, there's our notorious anti-elitism and instinctive suspicion of anyone perceived to be setting themselves up above the others. The physicist Ernest Rutherford, when asked why he returned so seldom to his native land, said that it was because it was the only place he ever went where all anyone wanted to discuss was what he'd got up to behind the bike sheds at school. Perhaps it's for this reason that so many of our writers, myself included, have chosen to publish under a pseudonym.

16

The dry sand had turned the corpse entrusted to its keeping into a yellow-brown mummy. I told Gunga Dass to stand off while I examined it. The body – clad in an olive-green hunting-suit much stained and worn, with leather pads on the shoulders – was that of a man between thirty and forty, above middle height, with light, sandy hair, long moustache, and a rough unkempt beard. The left canine of the upper jaw was missing, and a portion of the lobe of the right ear was gone. On the second finger of the left hand was a ring, a shield-shaped bloodstone set in gold, with a monogram that might have been either 'B.K.' or 'B.L.' On the third finger of the right hand was a silver ring in the shape of a coiled cobra, much worn and tarnished.

17

When my father died five years ago, he left behind a rather large and motley assortment of books, reflecting every transient stage in his interests: children's fiction, military history, local history, not to mention endless books about the sea. Many of them had been stored in an unlined, unheated building called 'the bookshed' out at the back of the property, and most of these were so perished and swollen with damp that they had to be disposed of by the local junk removal operatives. Black mould had started to grow on their spines. The remainder, after being sorted through by two second-hand book dealers, ended up in an old storeroom downstairs: somewhat dusty, but at least dry.

18

Among them was an almost complete set of the short stories of Rudyard Kipling – mostly in the 'Dominions' edition of 1913 – but with a couple of interesting rarities thrown in. One of these was an illustrated edition of *The Brushwood Boy*, a story from *Many Inventions* (1893). The other was an early American reprint of *The Phantom 'Rickshaw and other Eeerie Tales*, from the mid-1890s. Both of these I appropriated for my own use, leaving the others to await an uncertain fate downstairs. That may, in retrospect, have been a mistake. It's easy to be wise after the event, though. All I felt at the time was a certain satisfaction in saving these few relics from his once so extensive library.

19

I should explain, to start with, that Rudyard Kipling published eleven standalone 'official' collections of short stories. *The Phantom 'Rickshaw* appears in the third of these, *Wee Willie Winkie and other Stories* (1890). It collects three of the six small 'Indian Railway Library' paperbacks of his work published for local consumption between 1888 and 1889 (the other three are collected in *Soldiers Three*). Of course, Kipling published various other collections of stories, in America and Europe as well as in Great Britain, as well as many uncollected stories in anthologies and periodicals, but it's his final, collected edition, reflecting his mature intentions, that I'm speaking of here.

20

So much for preamble. I'd like you to note a few of the numbers above, though, for future reference: **11**, the number of authorised short story collections by Kipling; **13**, both the year of the 'Dominion' edition, and the total of his books left behind by my father, the eleven collections plus two separate volumes; **7**, the number of Indian Railway paperbacks published by Kipling in India between 1888 and 1889, when he left to return 'home' – also, incidentally, the number of years he spent working as a writer in India; finally, **6**, the number of 'trifles' recovered from the 'burrow' the dead white man was living in, as well as the number of novels by the 'divine Jane' [Austen] of his later war story 'The Janeites' (1924).

21

Kipling's relationship with the occult: ghosts, numerology, spiritualism, was always an uneasy one. It was his sister, Alice, known in the family as 'Trix', who became a medium, however, under the pseudonym 'Mrs. Holland'. The subject crops up again and again in his stories, sometimes as a vehicle for mockery, as in the thinly veiled attack on Madame Blavatsky – one of whose séances his father had attended when she first came to India in 1880 – in 'The Sending of Dana Da' (1888); sometimes with more serious intent as in 'The House Surgeon' (1909), or, for that matter, 'The Brushwood Boy' itself.

22

One of the strangest of all his stories, though, is also one of the earliest: 'The Strange Ride of Morrowbie Jukes', written when he was only 19, and published in *Quartette*, the Christmas Annual of the *Civil and Military Gazette* for 1885, which included four stories by Kipling, together with sundry items by his parents and sister. The story is strongly influenced by Poe and other nineteenth century writers of the macabre (Guy de Maupassant – his other great early influence – among them: 'Le Horla,' in particular). Yet it has an indisputable originality to it. The circumstantial nature of the descriptions is all Kipling, as is the emphasis on race and cultural prejudice. It has had its own influence, too, Borges's story 'The Immortal' clearly draws on it, and so, it has been claimed, does Sartre's play *Huis Clos*: No Exit.

23

The story is a simple one: An Englishman falls by accident down a sandbank and finds himself stranded in a strange community of people who have been condemned to stay there because they were proclaimed officially 'dead' at some point – either through disease or accident – and can therefore not be allowed to go back among the living. Any attempt to escape from the river bank they've been left on is prevented by a sniper in a boat, stationed in midstream, as well as by the quicksands that surround them. The protagonist, Morrowbie Jukes, meets an old servant of his, one Gunga Dass, who helps him initially, but then starts to lord it over him, in a reversal of the conventional hierarchies of the Raj.

24

Gunga Dass deposited a handful of trifles he had picked out of the burrow at my feet, and, covering the face of the body with my handkerchief, I turned to examine these. I give the full list in the hope that it may lead to the identification of the unfortunate man:

1. *Bowl of a briarwood pipe, serrated at the edge; much worn and blackened; bound with string at the crew.*
2. *Two patent-lever keys; wards of both broken.*
3. *Tortoise-shell-handled penknife, silver or nickel. name-plate, marked with monogram 'B.K.'*
4. *Envelope, postmark undecipherable, bearing a Victorian stamp, addressed to 'Miss Mon—' (rest illegible) —'ham' —'nt.'*

25

The body described in the quotations above reveals to Jukes that he is not the first 'white man' to fall victim to the strange superstitions of these Hindus, and he is just on the point of attempting a perilous escape through the quicksand when the timely intervention of one of his own servants enables him to scale the slippery sands at the edge of the colony. It's hard to convey the sheer horror of Kipling's descriptions of this strange community – a bit like a leper colony, but even more cut off from the world. It has something of Poe's 'Descent into the Maelstrom', no doubt, but surely it must have been based on either a nightmare or a real experience of the author's?

26

5. *Imitation crocodile-skin notebook with pencil. First forty-five pages blank; four and a half illegible; fifteen others filled with private memoranda relating chiefly to three persons – a Mrs. L. Singleton, abbreviated several times to 'Lot Single,' 'Mrs. S. May,' and 'Garmison,' referred to in places as 'Jerry' or 'Jack.'*
6. *Handle of small-sized hunting-knife. Blade snapped short. Buck's horn, diamond cut, with swivel and ring on the butt; fragment of cotton cord attached.*

It must not be supposed that I inventoried all these things on the spot as fully as I have here written them down. I conveyed [them] to my burrow for safety's sake, and there being a methodical man, I inventoried them.

27

Other interesting features of the story include the odd choice of names for his principal characters. Why 'Morrowbie Jukes,' for instance? The slightly Gallic sound to the name might support those commentators who have seen its closest avatar in Poe's 'The Facts in the Case of M. Valdemar,' a story Kipling references directly in his later piece 'In the House of Suddhoo'. Nor is it possible to encounter the name 'Gunga Dass' without a slight premonitory shiver for the future, faithful, fateful 'Gunga Din.' It's significant, too, that one of his many biographers, Angus Wilson, chose to adapt this title for his own account of Kipling's life: *The Strange Ride of Rudyard Kipling* (1977). He, at least, appears to have suspected something autobiographical in it.

28

But there's one extra, final paragraph in that old 'American Publishers Corporation' edition owned by my father:

> *To cut a long story short, Dunnoo is now my personal servant on a gold mohur a month – a sum which I still think far too little for the services he has rendered. Nothing on earth will induce me to go near that devilish spot again or to reveal its whereabouts more clearly than I have done. Of Gunga Dass I have never found a trace, nor do I wish to do. My sole motive in giving this to be published is the hope that someone may possibly identify, from the details and the inventory which I have given above, the corpse of the man in the olive-green shooting-suit.*

29

This *does* have the effect of bringing us back to the very circumstantial – and surely unnecessarily detailed nature of the description, quoted above, of the dead European. It's hard to avoid the idea, in fact, that some further communication is intended in this set of six items. Not, presumably, to the reader of today, but perhaps to some specific reader who might have been reached by *Quartette*. That surname 'Singleton' seems particularly suggestive, implying (as it does) a failed romance, leaving the two principals still 'single', foot loose and fancy-free. 'Jerry' (or 'Jack') Garmison is harder to identify at this date. There was, however, a seventeenth-century Jewish scholar called *Samuel* Garmison whose work on Spirit Possession in Judaism is still frequently cited to this day.

30

I got lost. Again. Foreign cities and me! Everything went pretty well at the lecture: it was a big group, but there were a bunch of visiting students there who offered opinions and actually understood what I was saying. When we divided them into groups in the second hour, this was a great help. It was very dark and cold by the time we'd finished, though, and I couldn't quite face the long walk home, especially as I'd come in by subway, so didn't quite know where to go. Accordingly, I asked one of the teacher's aides to show me the way back to the underground.

31

This went okay until I got to the point where one needed to switch between line four and line ten. I was about to go off in the wrong direction, when I thought again and looked at the map, and went all the way across to the other side to go the opposite way. Phew! But the subway station nearest my hotel has two almost identical exits onto different streets. I think it must have been this unfortunate fact that got me confused. I knew I had to go down the street, cross the road, and there the hotel would be. But there, alas, it wasn't.

32

So I retraced my steps and tried to go the other way. But that led back to a road marked on the map as being in the opposite direction. I went back once more, tried to imagine that I was coming out of the station for the first time, and set off again, crossing the road for the umpteenth time. But was it the right road? Nothing made any sense. It was very dark, and I'd been walking up and down for what seemed like hours by now. Eventually I found a security guard and showed him my print-out from google maps. He didn't understand it (most of it was in English), but pointed vaguely to the left of where we were standing.

33

At this a passer-by joined in: 'Are you all right?' he asked.

I allowed I wasn't.

'Where do you need to get to?'

'The Red Chamber Hotel.'

'Go left, across one big street, across another street for pedestrians, then another street, and it will be on your left. About ten minutes' walk.' I thanked him profusely and shook his hand, then followed his directions to the letter.

Sure enough, there it was: big and unmissable. As another of the teacher's aides said, though, everything is so much *farther* than you anticipate. Beijing is such a big place. Even getting to the subway station and back was almost too much for me. I think I might stick to guided tours from now on.

34

I've been counting it up on my fingers. Seven more sleeps. I suspect more like *six*, really, there's tonight, Thursday, Friday, then the long-drawn-out madness of the weekend, moving inexorably into Monday and finally departure on Tuesday night, whilst I sit here twiddling my thumbs and feverishly watching my way through the likes of *Highway Through Hell* and other classics. *Everything* about me seems to rile and irritate the people at this hotel. They have a desk for changing money, but it turns out not *my* kind of dollars when I asked them for a rate. For that I had to go to an outside bank, where I waited over an hour and a half to change fifty dollars, all I had on me.

35

I noticed some of the guests wearing their slippers in the dining room a day or two after I came, so decided to do the same. This morning there was a sign: 'Guests are asked not to wear their slippers in the restaurant.' Just a *little* passive-aggressive, don't you think? I went all the way back up to my room in the lift, put on some lace-up shoes, and came back down to have my pre-paid-for (thank God!) breakfast. I mean, what difference does it make? Why should one need to wear shoes just to move from floor to floor? It's not the thing itself, mind you, just the way it was done.

36

I've ordered room service a couple of times now, and the tray has been collected next day by housekeeping. Today there was a little note on it when it arrived asking me to ring the room service number to have the tray collected after I'd finished 'for your comfort and convenience.' When, however, I dutifully rang the number, they couldn't understand what I was talking about, and instead kept on asking what I wanted to order. The staff in general, I would say, are surly and suspicious and almost completely devoid of a desire to help with anything – the reverse of what I've encountered elsewhere.

37

The waiter who's brought
my room-service tray
two or three times
catches my eye
at breakfast

wanting to be recognised?
I'm not quick enough
so he turns back
disappointed
the others just scowl

38

I saw one other foreigner in the subway yesterday, and no others in Tiananmen Square. My colleague back home was right. They pay no attention to us. But any attention they *do* pay is mostly hostile, I feel: with occasional honourable exceptions such as the man who gave me directions home after my lecture, mind you. I *do* feel a different atmosphere here than in Shanghai, which seemed a much more cosmopolitan, outward-looking city. Here there are barriers and policemen everywhere and one hesitates to go down any byways for fear of being told off. I'll be awfully glad to be back home again.

39

I can't check it here anymore, of course – no Facebook in China – but shortly before I left I noticed my own Facebook page had 666 follows:

It's not that I saw this as particularly significant in itself. I'm not *that* crazy. Nor am I unaware of the fact the so-called 'Number of the Beast' tends to come up every time anyone indulges in a spot of numerology. I remember in *War and Peace* where Pierre has decided to assassinate Napoleon during his invasion of Russia, and takes comfort from the fact that *l'russe Besuhof* adds up to 666, just like *l'empereur Napoléon*. It's true that he has to drop (incorrectly) the 'e' from *le* to get this result, but he justifies it by analogy with the (correct) elision in *l'empereur*.

40

So I wasn't particularly alarmed when the 666 *follows* turned into 666 *likes* a few days later:

666 likes +7 this week

Why should one be so worried at these kinds of coincidences, anyway? They happen all the time. Synchronicity, Jung called it: an 'acausal connecting principle' in the structure of the universe. And, in any case, 7 is generally a *good* number, combining the Christian trinity with the four elements: there were seven days of creation, seven days in the week, seven colours in the rainbow, seven letters in the Roman numerical system (I, V, X, L, C, D, M), seven seas, seven seals in the *Book of Revelation*.

41

However, the seventh month in the lunar calendar is also the Ghost Month in Chinese folklore: paper money and offerings are burned to appease the hungry, wandering ghosts who are permitted to revisit the earth during this period. The best seats at concerts are reserved for ghosts, and the music is played at exceptionally high volume, so that they can hear it. On the fifteenth day a feast is held to persuade them to return to the underworld. Otherwise they may invade your house and bring bad luck. Interestingly enough, the seventh day of this seventh month is reserved for lovers.

42

According to tradition, that's because it's the one day in the year when the Jade Emperor permits his daughter to meet her own lover, a cowherd who stole her magic robe from her while she was bathing. When she found the robe where he'd hidden it, she took the opportunity to make a visit to her father, but to stop her going back to her lowly husband, the emperor diverted all the rivers of heaven to flow in between them, thus creating the milky way. Once in a year they are allowed to meet in the middle of a bridge over the stream.

43

My God, this is a strange country! None of my cards work in the machines here, so my cash is being whittled away at an alarming rate. The only place I can use a credit card seems to be here at the hotel and they're about as unhelpful as could be. There's a nice little office space here in the room, though, and I'm actually finding it quite a good place to work, making revisions to my lectures at the insistence of Tanchun, the Chinese NZ Centre contact here. I've added a whole load of new images to my Powerpoint presentation. If they want the full story from soup to nuts, they can certainly have it!

44

I *did* go out yesterday to explore the central city: took the subway to Tiananmen Square and had a bit of a wander around. The National Theatre is certainly a striking looking building. But I forgot to mention the one real success so far. The room was far too hot, so after a couple of days I rang up to ask about it, I'd already made various attempts to adjust the thermostat. They sent along someone from housekeeping who pointed triumphantly at the thermostat. I made various gestures designed to show that nothing one did to it actually lowered the temperature. So after a while she just went over and opened a window.

45

Triumph! Now, by judicious blending of the freezing air from outside and the scorching air inside, I can maintain something resembling a living temperature: a bit of Chinese practicality at work there. I have to say it did surprise me that the windows actually opened, but I've been very grateful for the information. *Surely* we're on the countdown now. The funny thing is that I thought I saw some movement out of the corner of my eye as I turned away from the window. I guess it was just the curtain fluttering, but for a moment I was sure that there was someone else in the room. The fruits of being on my own for so many days, I suppose. I'm definitely pretty high up in the tower here.

46

And now I'm *here*, sitting in the NZ Centre, having made my way there all by myself. two stops north on line four to East Gate of Peking University, one stop west on line ten towards Suzhou. This is quite impressive, when you consider how thoroughly lost I got last time. It was really quite shameful, though not entirely surprising. Going back will be harder than getting here, I fear. It's a spectacularly beautiful campus, for the oldest, and possibly most prestigious, university in China. Mao Tse-Tung was once the librarian here. There's a memorial to Edgar Snow down by the lake.

47

My plan is to go to the Great Wall tomorrow, and the Forbidden City possibly on Saturday. After that my tally will be complete, and no arseholes will be able to one-up me about their own Chinese travels. It may sound petty, but that is the way it is. Not that I have any bucket list nonsense going on in my head, but just a decent sense of seizing opportunities when they present themselves. I fear I'm disappointing Tanchun bigtime. She'd clearly prefer it if I attended lectures with the contingent of Canterbury students who are here with us. Not on your Nellie, though, I'm not here to listen to lectures on Chinese culture. There's enough of that kind of thing available at home.

48

Today, too, I took some photos really for the first time. It's good to chronicle places and people. I think. The latter are more difficult, as one can't simply snap, one must ask permission. Shortly I will lift my lordly arse into gear again, and start the painful business of making my way home. I feel that honour is satisfied so far as my duty-to-be-absent for housekeeping is concerned. They were unbelievably persistent on that first day when my only hope was to get some uninterrupted rest. The lecture holds fewer fears for me now. They seem a nice, responsive group, and I can pull out the stops a bit more so far as expanding on the texts – which they may even have read this time – is concerned.

49

Again, it seems like an awful long way to send me just to give two talks. Tanchun would rather I'd stayed till the end of the week so as to set up some meetings with other Academics in the literary sphere. Will they invite me back? I must confess I couldn't care less. Of course it would be infinitely simpler a second time, but my assumption is that they won't. I don't think it's really integral to their view of the subject as a whole. Tanchun is of another opinion. Even though her own field is history, she certainly seems to feel that my input has helped to liven up the course. Whatever *that* means. I *hope* something good, not another veiled insult disguised with soft soap.

50

11th Anniversary of her death. On the Great Wall. Surrounded by Francophones: '*Ah, un plat!*' They all seem determined to reach the summit. For me, this is sufficient, I think. I have to say it all looks very *recent*: the mortar, even a lot of the stone work. It's hard to convince oneself of the 'ancient-ness' of it all, especially as it's mostly Ming-built, according to the guide, Ping. Other interesting aspects:

1. Lots of graffiti in English, but often with Indian names attached – 2015 a popular date.
2. The mountain barrier makes Beijing very defensible – but also affects the climate somewhat adversely. This is one of the few valley-gaps in the wall, so is exceptionally heavily fortified.

51

As it turns out, it's just me on this particular guided tour of the Wall and the Ming Tombs in the valley nearby. I had no idea how steep it was! It was more like climbing a mountain by way of endless flights of stairs than strolling around a few battlements. There was a great sign halfway up:

> *Don't fight, pick quarrels and stir up trouble and gather to gamble feudal superstitions and other illegal activities are forbidden.*

I should think so too! All in all, it was very interesting, but this may have exhausted my taste for guided tours for the moment. You are rather at their mercy once you climb into the bus. The guide, Mrs. Ping, was very informative, though, and had a whole bunch of good ghost stories to impart.

52

I just sprang for a major piece of tourist kitsch: my own 'Great Wall' book with my picture in it: ¥100. Must economise! If they try to take me for some jade, it'll have to be paid for via the credit card. I don't know if it's really an epoch-making experience but at least now it's done. I suspect that they film on the other side of the valley: it is a bit precipitous for such niceties here. Annex: at the Jade factory. Just sprung $700 or so for two jade pendants and a 'happiness ball' – with dragons and phoenixes, and twelve holes for the twelve months – I did rather like it, I must say. Perhaps company for our bronze dragon back home. It is, after all, quite a *significant* anniversary: steel for strength, for hanging on regardless.

53

The Beijing subway closes down every night at 11 pm by arrangement with the ghosts. According to Ping, a monk talked to them for three days back in the 1970s after many accidents had taken place. Palaces used to be burned down to eliminate the ghosts, because they move so fast, hence the use of the colour red to represent flames, and thus good luck. One should step over the threshold of a tomb with the right leg if one is male: Males east, women west, if you imagine yourself facing south from the tomb. One must be *very* careful not to step through the back gate, as it marks the boundary between the two worlds.

54

There was a very comfortable looking black-and-white pussy cat lying slap in the middle of the courtyard of the first Ming Emperor's tomb. He didn't see any particular need to move when the guard came over, but as it turned out it was only to give him a pat. The rest of the layout was more or less as follows:

Wall – to guard against robbers, I suppose.

Courtyard – large, carefully aligned in the right directions.

Lions – female on the left (with cub), male on the right (with ball)

Temple – in this case, with an extensive collection of artefacts.

Gate – you can go back but not forward through this. If you *do* go back through it, you should laugh loudly and slap yourself to discourage the ghosts from coming with you.

Tower – to watch out for trouble.

Tomb – unexcavated, buried under a hillside of earth and trees.

55

From: shixiangyun

Dear Dr. —,

I'm Shi Xiangyun. Welcome to China!

It is my great honor to visit the Forbidden City with you. I will arrive at the lobby of the Red Chamber Hotel at half past eight to meet you. And then we can take the tube to the destination.

However, I must return to the school before lunch as a consequence of my class which is scheduled at three o'clock tomorrow. In order to compensate this, I would love to invite you to have lunch in my university.

I have to say that my spoken English is not such good. Maybe there will be some problems in our communication. But, I do believe we would have a good time!

By the way, it only take me ¥40 to buy your ticket. So ¥120 is not appropriate.

Looking forward to meeting you.

P.S. Please wear comfortable shoes because maybe tomorrow we will walk a long distance. And if the air condition is not so good, you 'd better wear a mask.

Sincerely,

Shi Xiangyun

56

I had a strange dream last night. I was working undercover for some shadowy government agency, with orders to infiltrate a cell of dissidents. This I did with fair success, but while there I gradually befriended a young woman who treated me, at first, with disdain, but gradually came to trust me more and more. We were on a train, I recall, going to some dramatic confrontation when her feelings became truly apparent. She sat down close to me, and started to confess a series of things about her former life, her ambitions to be a teacher or a writer, and some even more intimate revelations.

57

I felt a great warmth towards her. At once the parameters of my mission seemed to fade, and my fondness for her to surge up. I was just on the point of declaring my feelings when, all of a sudden, I woke up. As usual in such cases, the feeling of bereftness from the dream persisted for quite some time. The idea that it was now irrecoverable seemed more bitter even than usual. It made matters worse that the thing that awoke me was somebody pounding on the door. It took me some time to pull myself together and stumble over to the eyehole. Outside there was something of a deputation. A man in a suit, a uniformed maid, and one of the concierges from the front desk.

58

'What do you want,' I asked through the door. The concierge replied in such accented English that I couldn't at first understand him. After some time it became clear that he was asking for my date of birth.

'Why do you need that?' I riposted. He persisted, though, so finally I obliged. There was a brief silence on the other side of the door, then he started banging again, and demanding that I open up.

'But I'm not dressed,' I said.

'That doesn't matter. We need to come in. We'll call security if we have to.'

This last threat tipped the balance for me. I opened the door, and ushered them in, having taken the precaution of wrapping myself in one of their generic towelling bathrobes.

59

'You need to leave,' said the young concierge.

'What do you mean? I'm booked in here for … *my mind went blank here* … a few more days at least,' I finished, hastily.

'Your booking has run out. You need to leave. You need to be out by ten o'clock this morning.'

'But where shall I go? My flight isn't for … *once again details which had seemed at my fingertips a few moments before deserted me* … a few days. My company booked me in till then.'

At this point the man in the suit started to shout at me, his words translated simultaneously by the concierge: 'You must leave the hotel! We have no more booking for you!'

60

'But – I have a credit card, I can pay for a few more nights if you need me to.'

'No more nights in this room. You must leave by ten this morning.'

'But I'll have to find somewhere else to stay. Can't you give me a few more hours at least?'

'Till two this afternoon. But after that we'll be back with security, and you will be made to leave.' And so they departed.

The whole thing *does* seem odd. My first act was to check my hotel booking and flight reservations but they weren't there. I had them saved on my laptop, I thought, but there was nothing there when I checked.

61

As for the little plastic pouch I used for my tickets and other information, it was nowhere to be seen. My suitcase and clothes were there, a drift of tourist brochures and other paperwork, but there were no records of the duration of my booking here, or even the length of my overall stay. And yet I must have had them at *some* stage, or I couldn't have checked in in the first place. The problem is my memory, I think. I've been looking back through these notes, but not with much success, I must confess. They seem very disordered. And I don't really remember writing them, to tell you the truth.

62

I recall quite a lot of what's happened here, but these actual written records of them seem shadowy, distant from me – just how long *have* I been here? DID I MISS MY FLIGHT HOME? It's always been my nightmare, to miss that vital connection, be stranded in a foreign city where I don't speak the language, without friends or contacts, through simple forgetfulness of some crucial event or transfer. Is *that* what happened? I don't *recall* packing my suitcase, or planning my departure, booking a taxi, checking departure times from the airport, booking a shuttle back home. I can't simply have forgotten those things, can I?

63

The whole thing is certainly stranger than anything in my experience. Was it a mini-stroke, a small touch of amnesia striking me in the night, which has left me hanging on here past my date of departure? I don't really know who to ask, or how to act. All I know for certain is that I have only a few hours here in this room, with phones and connections, to plan my course of action to get out of here. If I do – what do I mean, of course I will, it's just a question of how – I'll do my level best never to get pushed into one of these situations again.

64

Why did they need me here in the first place? Surely pretty much *anyone* in my field could have accomplished the few small tasks I seem to have been sent here for. I don't quite remember what they were, right now, to be honest, but I'm sure that they've all been finished now – I *hope* satisfactorily. When I opened the laptop on my desk I found the following quote – from C. S. Lewis's old SF novel *That Hideous Strength*, it would appear:

> *'Who is called Sulva? What road does she walk? Why is the womb barren on one side? Where are the cold marriages?'*

65

Ransom replied,

> *'Sulva is she whom mortals call the Moon. She walks in the lowest sphere. Half of her orb is turned towards us and shares our curse. On this side the womb is barren and the marriages cold. There dwell an accursed people, full of pride and lust. There when a man takes a maiden in marriage they do not lie together, but each lies with a cunningly fashioned image of the other, made to move and to be warm by devilish arts, for real flesh will not please them, they are so dainty (delicate) in their dreams of lust. Their real children they fabricate by vile arts in a secret place.'*

66

I've *got* to get out of here. I hope they'll let me store my suitcase down below. There's a little door behind the front desk which I've seen them wheeling luggage out of, so perhaps my big bag can go in there. I wouldn't bet on it, though. They've taken of late to ignoring me when I go up to talk to them: not making eye contact, refusing to acknowledge I'm even speaking to them. But I do feel afraid to leave the hotel altogether. Where else could I go? The airport? So many security checks to go through, so many officials to placate.

67

No, I've spotted a little walk-in cupboard the cleaners use a few doors down from my room, up on the third floor. I don't see why I shouldn't slip in there. Nobody uses it most of the time, and when they do I'll just wander around like any other guest. No more free breakfasts, admittedly, but I doubt that they'll question my right just to sit here, in the lobby. After all, I *could* simply be waiting for my guests to arrive. Plenty of people do that here. They even have quite noisy colloquies in the middle of the floor, rough-looking fellows up here from the countryside, maybe just for the day, maybe for longer: the trip of a lifetime.

68

And I've seen *her* there already a couple of times. Pale and a bit sickly looking, a mask on her face to keep out the toxic dust, a scarf for warmth. Just as she was when she returned to campus for that fateful cup of tea. At first I just thought that it was a coincidence when I saw her there, right in the middle of the lobby, scrolling down her phone. It can't be! I thought. But it was. I haven't yet spoken to her, mind you. I'm waiting for her to make the first move. If I wait too long, the others may come, and that would ruin everything.

69

I wish, above all, I could remember her name. *Miss Mon*—' *(rest illegible)* —'*ham*' —'*nt.*' What's *that* when it's at home? Miss Moneypenny? Or Monkey, as in that *other* classic novel, *Journey to the West?* '—'ham" and '—'nt" seem a bit easier to me. The Hamilton Gardens back home include both a Chinese Scholars' and a Chinoiserie garden, not to mention the Indian Char Bagh garden, and one of their principal events each year is the Katherine Mansfield garden party – Kathleen Beau**ham**p, that is – whose work has been described as 'one of the great monume**nt**s of the world's literature.' Missed **Mon**ument, perhaps: like the one to Edgar Snow.

70

What I find myself remembering most is that tour of the forbidden city with young Xiangyun. She turned out to have been named after one of the characters in my favourite Chinese novel, the *Red Chamber Dream*. They call it 'Redology,' the study of each and every odd aspect of that strangest of novels. Mao Tse-Tung was a particular devotee of it, too, it seems. The hotel must have been named after it, I suppose. Strange that I never thought of that before. She was refreshingly frank about her future desires and ambitions as we walked through the seemingly endless courtyards and byways of that immense folly.

71

All her life, it appears, her dream had been to stroll by the banks of Weiming Lake as a university student. It was her definition of felicity. And now she'd achieved her goal! But somehow it didn't, now, seem enough. She needed another dream to motivate her forward, but the future seemed all hard work and study and nothing particular to look forward to. I tried to make light of it, encourage her to enjoy her triumph in simply having got here from her small home town: 'You must get fêted every-time you go home: surely you're the local folk hero?' As I turned to put a coin in one of the big brass vessels to wish her good luck, she stopped me and asked to look at it.

72

It was just a small coin from home which had been lurking unseen at the bottom of my old wallet: there was a tattooed face on it. It was quite shiny, though, and she asked if she could keep it.

'Of course you can,' I said. 'I only wish I had something more impressive to give you.'

'This will be fine,' she replied, saying she did perhaps still have the dream of foreign travel to look forward to.

'You must come and see me if you ever get over there,' I said, and she looked at me strangely. 'What *is* the name of your town, anyway?'

She said, 'It's near Harbin. The coldest place in the world. Every time I go back I get sick. Last time it lasted a month. I lay with my face to the wall.'

Kipling and the Cross-Correspondences

Amongst the founders of the British Society for Psychical Research in 1882 were psychologist Edmund Gurney (1847-1888), philosopher Henry Sidgwick (1838-1900) and classicist Frederic W. H. Myers (1843-1901).

It was hoped, not unreasonably, that these learned and dedicated pioneers in the field of parapsychology might make some concerted attempt to 'come through' after their deaths, given their sustained interest in the question of some kind of survival of bodily dissolution.

Myers' immense tome *Human Personality and Its Survival of Bodily Death* was published posthumously, in 1903. He certainly believed that he had provided in its pages both strong evidence for survival and for the existence of a soul.

The strange phenomenon of the 'cross-correspondences' (so-called) which unfolded over two decades, beginning with some automatic writing scripts by Cambridge Classics lecturer Margaret Verrall in 1901, is therefore either the strongest, albeit also one of the strangest, chains of evidence for human survival of bodily death, or else a colossal piece of delusion and self-deception afflicting some of the acutest minds of the time.

Essentially, by choosing your authority, you choose the view you will be encouraged to take of the story. If, for instance, you read Deborah Blum's *Ghost Hunters: William James and the Search for Scientific Proof of Life after Death* (2006), you will be left with a lingering sense of mystery and doubt surrounding the whole business.

If, however, you read Ruth Brandon's trenchant *The Spiritualists: The Passion for the Occult in the Nineteenth and Twentieth Centuries* (1983), you may be left wondering why anyone could ever take seriously so bizarre a congerie of frauds and misfits?

The essence of the cross-correspondences was that it involved different mediums, on different continents, who separately received obscure and apparently nonsensical scripts which, when pieced together, produced more-or-less complete statements from (allegedly) specific individuals on 'the other side.'

The three principal conduits for these scripts were Mrs. Verrall, mentioned above, together with her daughter Helen; Mrs. Winifred Tennant, disguised under her professional name 'Mrs. Willett'; and Mrs Alice Fleming, sister of Rudyard Kipling, who practised under the name of 'Mrs Holland', thanks mainly to family disapproval.

As well as these, there was also some involvement from William James's favourite medium Leonora Piper in America. This geographical range from the United States to India has undoubtedly contributed something to the continuing fascination that still surrounds this psychic *cause célèbre*. And yet, what do these supposed 'correspondences' actually amount to?

One of the earliest instances was noted by Alice Johnson, research officer of the Society for Psychical Research. While sorting through some of the papers held at their office in London, she noted some strange similarities between them:

> in one case, Mrs. Forbes' script, purporting to come from her son, Talbot, stated that he must now leave her, since he was looking for a sensitive who wrote automatically, in order that he might obtain corroboration of her own writing. Mrs. Verrall, on the same day, wrote of a fir-tree planted in a garden, and the script was signed with a sword and a suspended bugle. The latter was part of the badge of the regiment to which Talbot Forbes had belonged, and Mrs. Forbes had in her garden some fir-trees, grown from seed sent to her by her son. These facts were unknown to Mrs. Verrall.

Taken alone, this might easily pass for coincidence, especially since, as she went on to say, 'We have reason to believe that the idea of making a statement in one script complementary of a statement in another had not occurred to Mr. Myers in his lifetime, for there is no reference to it in any of his written utterances on the subject that I have been able to discover.' However, in aggregate, she found the phenomenon less easy to dismiss:

> Neither did those who have been investigating automatic script since his death invent this plan, if plan it be. It was not the

automatists themselves that detected it, but a student of their scripts; it has every appearance of being an element imported from outside; it suggests an independent invention, an active intelligence constantly at work in the present, not a mere echo or remnant of individualities of the past.

Another frequently mentioned example was the famous (or infamous) 'Hope, Star, and Browning' correspondence. In this case three mediums made independent allusions to the poetry of Robert Browning. As Jill Galvan describes it:

> First, Margaret Verrall wrote a script mentioning 'anagram' and containing the phrases 'rats star stars' and 'tears stare,' along with a second script with the word 'Aster,' which is both Greek for star and another anagram for tears and stare. Additionally, this second script contained a phrase beginning with the Greek word for passion and continuing, 'the hope that leaves the earth for sky — Abt Vogler for earth too hard that found itself or lost itself — in the sky.' The investigators took the phrase to be an allusion to Browning's 'Abt Vogler' (1864), specifically to line 78, 'The passion that left the ground to lose itself in the sky'; the script substitutes Browning's original skyward 'passion' with 'hope.' Then, a couple of weeks later, a script by Piper asked if Margaret Verrall had gotten the message about 'Hope Star and Browning.' Around the same time, Helen Verrall received a couple of scripts that each mentioned 'star' and featured a drawing of one, as well as [alluding] to Browning's 'Pied Piper of Hamelin' (1842), and one of these scripts also offered anagrams for star in 'arts' and 'rats.'

This is the case which so impressed occult investigator Colin Wilson. And it does, on the face of it, seem difficult to interpret except as a series of allusions to essentially the same matter. Though precisely what was meant to be conveyed remains unclear.

One explanation for this, however, may be supplied by the sheer difficulty of transmission of ideas when one has left the earthly plain. Or so the defunct Frederic Myers explained at a séance with fellow psychical researcher Sir Oliver

Lodge:

> Lodge, it is not as easy as I thought in my impatience ... Gurney
> says I am getting on first rate. But I am short of breath ... I am
> more stupid than some of those I deal with ... It is funny to hear
> myself talking when it is not myself talking. It is not my whole self
> talking. When I am awake I know where I am.

He stated further:

> We communicate an impression through the inner mind of the
> medium. It receives the impression in a curious way. It has to
> contribute to the body of the message; we furnish the spirit of it
> ... In other words, we send the thoughts and the words usually in
> which they must be framed, but the actual letters or spelling of the
> words is drawn from the medium's memory. Sometimes we only
> send the thoughts and the medium's unconscious mind clothes
> them in words.

Another explanation of the process came from another psychic researcher, Dr
Richard Hodgson, via American medium Leonora Piper:

> I find now difficulties such as a blind man would experience in
> trying to find his hat, and I am not wholly conscious of my own
> utterances because they come out automatically, impressed upon
> the machine [the medium's body] ... I impress my thoughts on the
> machine which registers them at random, and which are at times
> doubtless difficult to understand. I understand so much better the
> modus operandi than I did when I was in your world.

The last word, though, must remain with Myers:

> Oh, if I could only leave you the proof that I continue. Yet another
> attempt to run the blockade – to strive to get a message through.
> How can I make your hand docile enough – how can I convince
> them? I am trying, amid unspeakable difficulties. It is impossible

for me to know how much of what I send reaches you. I feel as if I had presented my credentials – reiterated the proofs of my identity in a wearisomely repetitive manner. The nearest simile I can find to express the difficulty of sending a message is that I appear to be standing behind a sheet of frosted glass, which blurs sight and deadens sound, dictating feebly to a reluctant and somewhat obtuse secretary. A feeling of terrible impotence burdens me. Oh it is a dark road.

On April 24, 1907, while in trance in the United States, ... Mrs [Leonora] Piper three times uttered the word *Thanatos*, a Greek word meaning 'death,' despite the fact that she had no knowledge of Greek. Such repetitions were often a signal that cross-correspondences were about to begin. But it had begun already. About a week earlier, in India, Mrs Holland [i.e.: Alice Kipling] had done some automatic writing, and in that script the following enigmatic communication had appeared: '*Mors* [Latin for death]. And with that the shadow of death fell upon his limbs.' On April 29th, in England, Mrs Verrall, writing automatically, produced the words: 'Warmed both hands before the fire of life. It fades and I am ready to depart.' This is a quotation from a poem by nineteenth-century English poet, Walter [Savage] Landor. Mrs Verrall next drew a triangle. This could be Delta, the fourth letter of the Greek alphabet. She had always considered it a symbol of death. She then wrote: '*Manibus date lilia plenis*' [give lilies with full hands]. This is a quotation from Virgil's *Aeneid*, in which an early death is foretold. This was followed by the statement: 'Come away, come away, *Pallida mors* [Latin for pale death],' and, finally, an explicit statement from the communicator: 'You have got the word plainly written all along in your writing. Look back.' The 'word,' or 'theme,' was quite obvious when these fragments, given in the same month to three mediums thousands of miles apart, were put together and scrutinized. And in view of the lifelong interest of

Alice Fleming (née Kipling) (1868-1948)

the communicator, it was certainly an appropriate theme. Death.
— *Trans4mind*

When asked whether there was any basis to spiritualism, Kipling replied 'There is; I know. Have nothing to do with it.'
— George M. Johnson. *Mourning and Mysticism in First World War Literature and Beyond: Grappling with Ghosts* (2015)

Rudyard Kipling's famous poem 'En-dor' (1919) warns sternly of the dangers of false comfort from spirits, or rather, their dubious lieutenants, mediums:

> The road to En-dor is easy to tread
>> For Mother or yearning Wife.
> There, it is sure, we shall meet our Dead
>> As they were even in life.
> Earth has not dreamed of the blessing in store
> For desolate hearts on the road to En-dor.

He himself was no stranger to the subject. The death of his son John in combat at the Battle of Loos in 1915 was a blow he never really recovered from. It was made worse by the fact that he had had to exert all his special influence to ensure that John would be allowed to serve. He had already been rejected for active service due to his poor eyesight.

His poem 'My Boy Jack,' though ostensibly about the drowned dead of the Battle of Jutland, seems to refer obliquely to his own grief, also:

> 'Have you news of my boy Jack?'
>> *Not this tide.*
> 'When d'you think that he'll come back?'
>> *Not with this wind blowing, and this tide.*

> 'Has any one else had word of him?'
>> *Not this tide.*
> *For what is sunk will hardly swim,*
>> *Not with this wind blowing, and this tide.*
> 'Oh, dear, what comfort can I find?'

There's an almost Modernist fragmentedness about the gradual breakdown of the ballad form in this poem, a grief too great for the traditional forms Kipling had hitherto been sedulous in preserving.

If you want some sense of the contemporary atmosphere of a kind of half-life lived in the shadow of these immense crowds of thronging war dead, Charles Sturridge's 1997 film *Fairy Tale*, about the strange saga of the Cottingley Fairies, does a wonderful job of conveying it. Virtually all the literature of the time, the immediate post-war era – not simply such obvious examples as Eliot's *Waste Land* or Pound's 'Hugh Selwyn Mauberley' – should be read with this in mind.

Kipling's own short stories and poems chart his own steadily less unavailing attempts to come to term with his own intolerable loss. From the harsh 'Mary Postgate' (1915) he moved through the healing mechanisms of 'A Madonna of the Trenches' and 'The Janeites' (both 1924) to his most emotional and heartbreaking story of all, 'The Gardener' (1925).

John Radcliffe & John McGivering's 2011 notes on 'En-dor', the Kipling Society website, record the history of Kipling's engagements with spiritualism and the occult in general.

This ranges from his early story 'The Sending of Dana Da' (*Plain Tales from the Hills*, 1888), inspired by his father's scepticism about the claims of Madame Blavatsky, one of whose séances John Lockwood Kipling attended in 1880, to 'They' (1904), whose unnamed narrator suggests that the company of the dead may be permitted to those who have not known them in life, but not to those who, like himself, are searching for a particular dead child. This story appears to have been inspired by the death from pneumonia of Kipling's elder daughter Josephine, or 'Josie' (1892-1899).

Kipling was, it seems, only too aware of the presence in himself of something resembling the 'second sight' common among the MacDonalds, on his mother's side of the family. He wrote sceptically of this ability in his autobiography, *Something of Myself* (1937), but is careful, if one reads between the lines, not so much to deny its existence as to disavow its usefulness to the living:

there is a type of mind that dives after what it calls 'psychical experiences.' And I am in no way 'psychic.' Dealing as I have done with large, superficial areas of incident and occasion, one is bound to make a few lucky hits or happy deductions. But there is no need to drag in the 'clairvoyance,' or the rest of the modern jargon. I have seen too much evil and sorrow and wreck of good minds on the road to Endor to take one step along that perilous track.

Any unbiassed reader of his work will find it difficult to ignore the obvious fascination with telepathy, precognition, and other paranormal gifts which lies behind such stories as 'Wireless' (1902), 'The Wish House' (1924) and (perhaps most autobiographical of all) 'The House Surgeon' (1909).

Nor would it be true to say that the perils of the 'Road to En-dor' were more apparent to him after the First World War than before it. His simultaneous attraction-repulsion towards the occult seems to date from all stages of his career as a writer.

There are no reliable accounts of his own return from beyond the grave to answer any of the many questions raised by his works. His own comment on that is unequivocal. His late poem 'The Appeal' – first published in 1939 – reads as follows:

> If I have given you delight
>> By aught that I have done,
> Let me lie quiet in that night
>> Which shall be yours anon:
>
> And for the little, little, span
>> The dead are born in mind,
> Seek not to question other than
>> The books I leave behind.

The fear of such 'unknown forces' was certainly great in Rudyard Kipling, but the temptation to write about them was evidently greater.

His younger sister Alice, known to the family as 'Trix,' who shared with him the appalling experiences of child-abuse and neglect, recorded in his classic story 'Baa Baa Black Sheep' (1888), which occurred when they were sent 'home' to England from India in 1870, and who showed almost equal literary promise in her youth, took a rather different approach.

On her return to India at the age of sixteen, she married British army officer, John Fleming, and, in 1893, 'initially experimented with automatic writing.' Her biography in the *Encyclopedia of Occultism and Parapsychology* remarks somewhat euphemistically:

> After a long illness she returned to England in 1902 and in the following year read the classic study *Human Personality and Its Survival of Bodily Death*, by F. W. H. Myers. As a result she contacted the secretary of the Society for Psychical Research (SPR), London, regarding her own automatic writing.

This 'long illness' is presumably the 'recurrent mental illness' referred to in Radcliffe and McGivering's notes on her brother's poem 'En-dor' (quoted above), which overtook her in 'her thirtieth year'.

Trix's family linked her madness with her psychic interests. When asked whether he thought there was anything in spiritualism, Rudyard Kipling replied 'with a shudder,' 'There is; I know. Have nothing to do with it.' He is presumed to have been thinking of his sister.

The Society for Psychical Research appears to have treated her abilities equally seriously, but rather more analytically, as is evidenced by a series of papers on the 'cross-correspondences' controversy published by their research officer Alice Johnson in the Society's *Proceedings*:

- 'On the Automatic Writing of Mrs. Holland.' *Proceedings of the Society for Psychical Research* 21 (1908).
- 'Supplementary Notes on Mrs. Holland's Scripts.' *Proceedings* ... 22 (1909).
- 'Second Report on Mrs. Holland's Script.' *Proceedings* ... 24 (1910).
- 'Third Report on Mrs. Holland's Scripts.' *Proceedings* ... 25 (1911).

Then, as now, we are left with a stark choice: either to follow the hints, the half-stated truths 'known to nobody else', and the endlessly frustrating lack of definitive, convincing evidence of 'survival' – or else to reject the whole business as cruel deception on the part of 'sensitives' together with wish-fulfilment on the part of the client. Dr Johnson perhaps summed it up best, when remarking of ghosts:

> It is wonderful that five thousand years have now elapsed since the creation of the world, and still it is undecided whether or not there has ever been an instance of the spirit of any person appearing after death. All argument is against it; but all belief is for it.

> – Boswell: *Life of Johnson* (1791)

And yet, and yet thirty years before, in *Rasselas* (1759) he had commented with almost equal cogency:

> That the dead are seen no more ... I will not undertake to maintain, against the concurrent and unvaried testimony of all ages and all nations. There is no people, rude or learned, among whom apparitions of the dead are not related and believed. This opinion, which perhaps prevails as far as human nature is diffused, could become universal only by its truth; those that never heard of one another would not have agreed in a tale which nothing but experience can make credible. That it is doubted by single cavillers can very little weaken the general evidence; and some who deny it with their tongues confess it by their fears.

'Some who deny it with their tongues, confess it by their fears.' Kipling was very afraid of mental disturbances in the late 1890s, in the middle of a devastating quarrel with one of his wife's brothers, the 'unstable' Beatty Balestier, which threatened to undermine his and Carrie's experiment of living in the United States.

His sister's mental illness, followed swiftly by the death of the Kiplings' daughter Josie, must have constituted a great temptation to give in to what Sigmund Freud, in 1910, referred to as 'the black tide of mud of occultism.'

That temptation is already achingly strong in the story 'They,' and after John's avoidable death ten years later at the Battle of Loos, it may have seemed almost overwhelming.

The poem 'En-Dor,' then, is simply one instalment in that ongoing struggle with himself and with circumstances. For all the cogency of its description of spiritualism, one can't avoid the fact that – unlike Robert Browning, whose 'Mr. Sludge, 'The Medium' (1864) comes from a place of total non-belief – Kipling's resistance to communication with the dead seems to arise more from his conviction of its dangers to the living than from any inherent improbability in its claims:

> Whispers shall comfort us out of the dark —
> Hands — ah, God! — that we knew!
> Visions and voices — look and hark! —
> Shall prove that the tale is true,
> And that those who have passed to the further shore
> May be hailed — at a price — on the road to En-dor.
>
> But they are so deep in their new eclipse
> Nothing they say can reach,
> Unless it be uttered by alien lips
> And framed in a stranger's speech.
> The son must send word to the mother that bore,
> Through an hireling's mouth. 'Tis the rule of En-dor.

And what better summary of the cross-correspondences themselves can be found than the one contained in the following stanza?

> Even so, we have need of faith
> And patience to follow the clue.
> Often, at first, what the dear one saith
> Is babble, or jest, or untrue.
> (Lying spirits perplex us sore
> Till our loves — and their lives — are well-known at
> En-dor)....

'All argument is against it; but all belief is for it.' Quite so. There are no atheists in foxholes, as the saying has it. It's not that the question is, or, it seems ever can be, definitively settled. But I think Ursula Le Guin was right to say, in the third book of her 'Earthsea' series, *The Farthest Shore*:

the counsel of the dead is not profitable to the living

Rudyard Kipling, I suspect, would have agreed with her wholeheartedly.

Notes & Sources:

Epigraph

- *when a house is haunted* – Cao Xueqin, *The Story of the Stone*. 5 vols. *Volume 3: The Warning Voice*. Trans. David Hawkes (Harmondsworth: Penguin Classics, 1980), 425.

The Classic New Zealand Ghost Story
[Published in *The Imaginary Museum* (25/7/16): http://mairangibay.blogspot.com/2016/07/the-classic-new-zealand-ghost-story.html]

- *When I first started writing about apparitions* – Andrew Mackenzie, *Hauntings and Apparitions: An Investigation of the Evidence*. 1st ed. 1982 (London: Granada, 1983), 254.
- *the dark, threatening land* – *Cinema of Unease: A Personal Journey by Sam Neill* (NZ, 1995): https://www.nzonscreen.com/title/cinema-of-unease-1995.
- *What great gloom* – Allen Curnow, 'House and Land.' *Early Days Yet: New and Collected Poems 1941-1997* (Auckland: Auckland University Press, 1997), 234-35.

Stories

- *My mind on other things* – Peter Straub, *Ghost Story*. 1st ed. 1979 (London: Futura, 1980), 216.

Eketahuna
[Published in *Influence and Confluence: East and West. A Global Anthology on the Short Story*. Ed. Maurice A. Lee. Shanghai: East China Normal University Press, 2016. 388-95.]

The Scam
[Published as 'Hong Kong – 2001' in *brief* 25 (2002): 13-16.]
- *Open to experience* – Kendrick Smithyman, *Tomarata*. Ed. Peter Simpson (Tamaki: Holloway Press, 1996), [9].

Featherston
[Published in *Starch* 1 (2011): 71-74.]

Leaves from a Diary of the End of the World
[Published in *brief* 53 (2015): 80-97. 'Lacandon-Maya Poem,' 'Tzotzil-Maya Prayer,' and 'Yucatán-Maya Hunting Song' were published in

brief 49 (2013): 60-65.]

- *The world was so recent* – Gabriel García Márquez, *One Hundred Years of Solitude*. 1st ed. 1967. Trans. Gregory Rabassa, 1970 (London: Picador 1980), 9.
- *This legendary catastrophe* – 'Ancient 'Lizard People' Underground In LA?' *Reptoid.com*: http://www.reptoids.com/Vault/Schufeltsearch.htm.
- *The Maya wise men* – Michael Coe, *Breaking the Maya Code* (London: Thames and Hudson Ltd., 1982), 275-76.
- *in the Emerald City* – L. Frank Baum, *Journeys through Oz: The Wonderful Wizard of Oz & The Marvelous Land of Oz*. 1st eds 1900 & 1904. Illustrations by W. W. Denslow & John R. Neill (Leicester: Galley Press, 1982), 35.
- *Exceedingly little is known* – Michael Coe, *The Maya*. 1st ed. 1966. (London: Thames and Hudson Ltd., 2011), 223-24.
- *Oxlajuj B'aqtun: not the end* – University of Auckland website:http://www.arts.auckland.ac.nz/uoa/home/events/template/event_item.jsp?cid= 547350.
- *At the beginning of the road* – García Márquez, *One Hundred Years of Solitude*, 46.
- *'Dear me!' said Jack. 'I'm getting confused* – Baum, *The Marvelous Land of Oz*, 35.

Is it Infrareal or is it Memorex?

[Published in *Landfall* 230 (November 2015): 89-96.]

- *Someone had to call Ulises's mother* – Roberto Bolaño, *The Savage Detectives*. 1st ed. 1998. Trans. Natasha Wimmer, 2007 (London: Picador, 2009), 321.
- *Our visceral realist activities* – Bolaño, *Savage Detectives*, 196.
- *The night before* – Bolaño, *Savage Detectives*, 72.
- *At Don Crispin's request* – Bolaño, *Savage Detectives*, 101-2.
- *The review … tried to sum up* – Roberto Bolaño, *2666*. 1st ed. 2004. Trans. Natasha Wimmer, 2008 (London: Picador., 2009), 27-28.
- *There was something revelatory* – Bolaño, *2666*, 227.

Company

[Published in *An Encounter in the Global Village: Selected Stories from the 14th International Conference on the Short Story in English (English-Chinese)*. Ed. Hengshan Jin. Shanghai: East China Normal University Press, 2016. 366-77.]

General Grant in Paeroa

[Published in *brief* 56 (2018): 97-107.]

- *For David* – Bruce Catton, *Grant Takes Command*. 1st ed. 1969 (London: J. M. Dent & Sons Limited, 1970), vii.
- *I am informed that* – 'Te Kooti at Paeroa, Ohinemuri.' *New Zealand Herald*,

Vol. XX, Issue 6744 (29 June 1883), 5. *Papers Past*:
https://paperspast.natlib.govt.nz/newspapers/NZH18830629.2.39.

Brothers
[Published in *brief* 54 (2016): 99-104.]

- *Thick as Autumnal leaves* – John Milton, *Paradise Lost*, 11.302-3. Quoted from *Paradise Lost*. Ed. Alastair Fowler. 1968. Longman Annotated English Poets (London: Longman Group Limited, 1974), 62.
- *Methought I saw my late espousèd Saint* – John Milton, Sonnet XIX. Quoted from *Complete Shorter Poems*. Ed. John Carey. Longman Annotated English Poets. 1st ed. 1968 (London: Longman Group Limited, 1971), 413.
- *I've read* Phantasms of the Living – Edmund Gurney, Frederick W. H. Myers & Frank Podmore, *Phantasms of the Living*. 2 vols (London: Rooms of the Society for Psychical Research / Trübner & Co., 1886).
- *wherein all the Beasts of the Forest do move* – Psalms 104: v. 20 (Anglican Prayerbook version): quoted in 'Mr. Humphrey and His Inheritance.' *The Collected Ghost Stories of M. R. James*. 1st ed. 1931. Pocket Edition (London: Edward Arnold (Publishers) Ltd., 1964), 340.

Catfish
[Published in *The Radiance of the Short Story: Short Fiction from around the Globe*. Ed. Maurice A. Lee & Aaron Penn. Lisboa: Editora Edições Humus, Lda, 2018. 551-58.]
- *'Zac' in Geoff Murphy's 1985 film* – The Quiet Earth, dir. Geoff Murphy, writ. Bill Baer, Bruno Lawrence, Sam Pillsbury (based on the novel by Craig Harrison) – with Bruno Lawrence, Alison Routledge, Pete Smith – (NZ, 1985).
- *I had glimpsed, briefly* – Craig Harrison, *The Quiet Earth* (Auckland: Hodder & Stoughton, 1981), 82-83.
- *I know what I saw* – Harrison, *Quiet Earth*, 84.
- *put the muzzle of the shotgun* – Harrison, *Quiet Earth*, 85.

The Cross-Correspondences: Paragraphs
[Unpublished]

- *Lean near to life* – Max Beerbohm, 'Enoch Soames: A Memory of the Eighteen-nineties.' *Seven Men*. 1st ed. 1919 (London: William Heinemann Ltd., 1926), 11.
- *'fake it 'til you make it'* – 'The Apprentice: Martha Stewart.' *Wikipedia* (16/1/19): https://en.wikipedia.org/wiki/The_Apprentice:_Martha_Stewart.
- *The dry sand had turned* – Rudyard Kipling, *The Phantom 'Rickshaw and other Tales*. 1st ed. 1889 (New York: American Publishers Corporation, 1895),

75-76.

- *Gunga Dass deposited a handful* – Kipling, *The Phantom 'Rickshaw*, 76.
- *Imitation crocodile-skin notebook* – Kipling, *The Phantom 'Rickshaw*, 77.
- *To cut a long story short* – Kipling, *The Phantom 'Rickshaw*, 84.
- *a seventeenth-century Jewish scholar called* Samuel *Garmison* – 'Samuel Garmison.' *Wikipedia* (22/7/16): https://en.wikipedia.org/wiki/Samuel_Garmison.
- 'Who is called Sulva?' – C. S. Lewis, *The Cosmic Trilogy: Out of the Silent Planet; Perelandra; That Hideous Strength.* 1st eds 1938, 1943, 1945 (London: The Bodley Head, 1990), 551.

Kipling and the Cross-Correspondences

[Published in *The Imaginary Museum* (18/1/19): https://mairangibay.blogspot.com/2019/01/kipling-and-cross-correspondences.html]

- *in one case* – 'Cross-Correspondence.' *Encyclopedia of Occultism and Parapsychology* (2001). *Encyclopedia.com* (27/1/19): https://www.encyclopedia.com/science/encyclopedias-almanacs-transcripts-and-maps/cross-correspondence.
- *First, Margaret Verrall wrote a script* – Jill Galvan, 'Tennyson's Ghosts: The Psychical Research Case of the Cross-Correspondences, 1901-c.1936.' (July 2012). *BRANCH: Britain, Representation and Nineteenth-Century History*. Ed. Dino Franco Felluga. Extension of Romanticism and Victorianism on the Net. (27/1/19): http://www.branchcollective.org/?ps_articles=jill-galvan-tennysons-ghosts-the-psychical-research-case-of-the-cross-correspondences-1901-c-1936.
- *Lodge, it is not as easy as I thought* – Michael Tymn, 'Difficulties in Spirit Communication Explained.' *White Crow Books* (16/4/12): http://whitecrowbooks.com/michaeltymn/entry/difficulties_in_spirit_communication_explained.
- *Oh, if I could only leave you the proof* – Peter Shepherd, ed., 'Frederic Myers – Proof of Life After Death: Excerpts about the life of Frederick Myers from the book by Ian Currie 'You Cannot Die: The Incredible Findings of a Century of Research on Death'.' *Trans4mind* (27/1/19): https://trans4mind.com/spiritual/myers1.html.
- *Alice Fleming (née Kipling)* – 'Medium Alice Holland, England. UK, or Medium Alice MacDonald, or Medium Alice [Trix] Fleming, Medium Alice Kipling, Alice Holland, Alice Kipling,' *Psychic Truth Info* (27/1/19): http://psychictruth.info/Medium_Alice_Holland.htm.
- *On April 24, 1907, while in trance* – Shepherd, 'Frederic Myers.' *Trans4mind*.
- *When asked whether* – Quoted John Radcliffe & John McGivering. 'En-dor.' *Notes* (12/7/11): http://www.kiplingsociety.co.uk/rg_endor1.htm
- *The road to En-dor* – Rudyard Kipling, 'En-dor.' *The Cambridge Edition of the Poems of Rudyard Kipling*. Ed. Thomas Pinney. 3 vols (Cambridge:

Cambridge University Press, 2013), II: 1094-95.

- *'Have you news* – Rudyard Kipling, '"My Boy Jack".' *The Cambridge Edition of the Poems of Rudyard Kipling*. Ed. Thomas Pinney. 3 vols (Cambridge: Cambridge University Press, 2013), II: 1098.
- *there is a type of mind* – Rudyard Kipling, *Something of Myself: For My Friends Known and Unknown*. 1st ed. 1937. Ed. Robert Hampson. Introduction by Richard Holmes (Harmondsworth: Penguin, 1987), 160.
- *If I have given* – Rudyard Kipling, 'The Appeal.' *The Cambridge Edition of the Poems of Rudyard Kipling*. Ed. Thomas Pinney. 3 vols (Cambridge: Cambridge University Press, 2013), II: 461.
- *initially experimented with automatic writing* – 'Alice Kipling Fleming (1868-1948).' *Encyclopedia of Occultism and Parapsychology* (2001). *Encyclopedia.com* (27/1/19):https://www.encyclopedia.com/people/philosophy-and-religion/other-religious-beliefs-biographies/alice-kipling-fleming.
- *a series of papers on the 'cross-correspondences' controversy* – "Alice Kipling Fleming (1868-1948).' *Encyclopedia of Occultism and Parapsychology*.
- *it is wonderful* – James Boswell, *Boswell's Life of Johnson*. 1st ed. 1791. 4 vols Oxford: Talboys and Wheeler / London: William Pickering, 1826), III: 206 [1778].
- *That the dead are seen no more* – Samuel Johnson, *The History of Rasselas, Prince of Abissinia*. 1st ed. 1759 (New York: Dover Publications, Inc., 2005), 62.
- *he black tide of mud of occultism* – Nándor Fodor, *Freud, Jung, and Occultism* (New York: University Books, Inc., 1971), 206.
- *The counsel of the dead* – Ursula Le Guin, *The Farthest Shore*. 1st ed. 1972. *The Books of Earthsea: The Complete Illustrated Edition*. Illustrated by Charles Vess (USA: Saga Press, 2018), 300.

About Jack

Jack Ross works as a senior lecturer in creative writing at Massey University. He is the author of five poetry collections, four novels and three books of short fiction. His novel *The Annotated Tree Worship* was highly commended in the 2018 NZ Heritage Book Awards. He has also edited numerous books, anthologies, and literary journals, including *brief*, *Landfall*, and *Poetry New Zealand*. He blogs at mairangibay.blogspot.com